I0664410

After the Storm
by Nisia Skyy

DYNAMIC IMAGE PUBLICATIONS

Dynamic Image Publications

Copyright 2017 @ Tanisia Moore

Book cover design by Julian Gladness.

Photography by Tosha Gaines Photography.

Editing by Christian Cashelle.

Manufactured in the United States of America.

ISBN-13: 978-0-9894423-6-7
ISBN-10:   0-9894423-6-5

To my daughters, Syd and Savvy, thank you both for being my inspiration. Mommy loves you.

Prologue

Spring 2002

"Are you sure that you ready for this?" Rashad seductively asked Brooke.

Brooke gently squeezed her almond-shaped eyes closed and nodded her long head slowly. Rashad softly grabbed her face before giving her another passionate kiss and laying her down on the bed.

It was the night of their senior prom at North Dallas High School. They were now naked in a room at the W Hotel downtown. Earlier that evening, they were voted as prom queen and king. After the crowning, they danced the night away with their closest friends and anxiously awaited the very moment that was before them.

They'd both talked about this moment for the past few months and decided that this was going to be the night they would lose their virginity to each other. After all, they'd been dating for the past two years and were deeply in love. Rashad knew that one day he was going to marry Brooke after they both graduated from college and settled into their respective careers. She was the only person he could trust with any- and everything. She never criticized him the way his football coaches did if he missed a play. Or the way his father, the Bishop Michael Wallace, did when he failed to live up to his "holier than thou" standard way of living. Although he was eighteen, Rashad knew without a shadow of a doubt that Brooke was the one for him.

He could not believe that this special moment was actually happening.

Brooke lay on the bed and watched as Rashad went to get the condoms out of his overnight bag. As he bent over, she giggled at his behind which looked like a little black moon. Her giggling stopped the moment he started walking back toward the bed. She admired his naked six-foot-two body which reminded her of D'Angelo's in his popular video. She kept her anxious dark brown eyes on his confident dark brown eyes. Once he reached the bed, he confidently displayed his signature dimpled smile— showing off his straight pearly whites which only accented his flawless chocolate skin.

"What happens after this?" she asked as Rashad sat down next to where she was lying on the bed.

He could tell that she was nervous. If he was honest with himself, he was scared out of his mind because he wanted her to be pleased with his performance. But before answering her, he took a moment to regard her beauty. Brooke was the only girl at the prom who didn't wear a weave. Instead, she wore her Nia Long-inspired short haircut, which framed her long face perfectly. She had washed her face before coming to bed and a few acne scars were now visible. Even with the scars, her mocha skin was still smooth.

The bed covers hid her five-foot-four shapely body that was toned from her running track since their freshmen year.

"Well, Miss Jones," he said slowly while rubbing his hand against one of her perky nipples, "We go to Disneyland!"

"Rashad! You know what I mean, crazy."

They laughed and he kissed her again with just as much passion as he'd done earlier.

"No, seriously baby," he said, breaking their kiss. "Nothing changes after this happens. This is something we both want. But most importantly, we love each other."

"But we're going to different schools and you're leaving a few weeks after graduation for football camp. How are we going to sustain all fours years of college with your football schedule and our school work?"

"Brooke, you're worrying too much. We can only take each day at a time. I know my schedule is going to be crazy at UGA, but I'm going to be coming home every chance I get. I don't know why you didn't apply to any of the schools in Georgia."

"You know why. I'm going to be stuck right here going to Texas Southern like the rest of my family. Oh, and babysitting my two little sisters."

Brooke laid back down on the bed and briefly thought about how sick and tired she was of her parents planning her life. Little did her parents know, she too was accepted to UGA and Emory University with full scholarships to both. She knew her parents would never let her go to an out-of-state school, especially if her sole reason was to follow behind Rashad which would have been half true. But she really wanted to get out of the state of Texas!

Brooke wanted to start this new chapter of her life on her own terms and not on the terms of her parents. She knew they meant well, but at what point were they going to allow her to live her life as she pleased? It's not as if they hadn't accomplished great things in their own lives. Her mother was the principal at Rusk Middle School and her father was a partner with Rashad's mother at one of the largest law firms in Dallas.

Brooke knew the real reason they were so strict. Her parents didn't want her to make the same mistakes they made when they were her age. Brooke's mother had followed her father to Texas Southern and by the end of their freshman year, she was pregnant with Brooke. Her parents had been blessed that both sets of grandparents were willing to help raise her in order for them to complete their studies. This was the reason Brooke's parents preached about avoiding serious relationships with anyone and to preferably lose her virginity when she gets married. They told her there were no consequences for waiting on her husband but there would definitely be consequences if she didn't.

Again, she knew they meant well. While they could tell her what school she could attend, they couldn't tell Brooke that Rashad wasn't going to be her husband. It was this thought that made her give him the look, letting him know that she was ready to get this show on the road.

Brooke lay on her back looking at the ceiling. Rashad was trying to catch his breath as he wrapped his strong arms around her body to pull her closer to him. He gave her a loving kiss on her cheek and smiled with pure satisfaction. No longer a boy, he had become a man in a matter of a few minutes.

Gently grabbing Brooke's face to turn toward him, Rashad asked, "So, how was it, babe?"

Not quite sure how to answer, Brooke smiled at him but no words came out. She wasn't sure if what happened a mere five minutes ago counted as sex. The entire act; foreplay and penetration, lasted five minutes and not the hours as her friends said it would.

The foreplay had started out with kissing and heavy petting. Wanting to try out the moves they saw in adult films, they tried a sixty-nine. Epic fail! Poor Brooke accidentally scraped her teeth against Rashad's penis, which caused him to react by biting her vagina. Needless to say, the foreplay was over before it really began but they were both determined to continue the night and proceed to make love.

Rashad was able to place the Trojan magnum condom on with finesse, but the actual penetration was anything but. Trying to be gentle and ease his manhood into Brooke proved to be difficult. She cried from the pain of him trying to enter and told him, "Just stick it in there."

Afraid of hurting her any further, Rashad shoved his penis in as quickly as he could, which only caused her to scream from pain.

As he moved in and out of her, Brooke began to relax and enjoy. The moment she did, Rashad closed his eyes, announced that he was coming, and with a loud grunt, he was done. Brooke looked at the clock to notice only three minutes had passed since actual penetration.

"It was great, babe," she finally said and leaned over to give him a kiss on the lips.

Rashad gave a satisfying smile at her response and they talked until they fell asleep in each other's arms.

Part 1
The Calm

Chapter 1

Brooke

Summer 2010

"Great as always," Donovan said with a kiss to my forehead.

Donovan, Dee, or "Dee Money" as he called himself, was a self-proclaimed Atlanta rapper and my boyfriend of three years. I was at his apartment and we had just wrapped up having sex. As usual, he was all smiles and I was pretty disgusted.

Lately, I've been feeling very guilty after having sex with him. It was almost as if there was something telling me that I could do better. More like screaming, "Girl, what the hell is wrong with you?" I usually ignored that feeling, but today it seemed to be very loud and clear. Instead of stroking his ego, I got out of the bed and headed for the shower.

"Babe, you okay?" he asked as he came in the bathroom behind me.

"God, why does he bother my soul so much?" I thought to myself. I responded dryly to his query. "I'm fine, Dee."

"Then why are you acting all weird and sh—?"

"Watch it!"

Donovan flushed the toilet and went over to the sink to wash his hands. Once he left the bathroom, I allowed my tears to fall freely from my eyes. I made sure not to cry loudly and attract him back into the bathroom. I found myself constantly doing this after sex. It was as if my soul needed to release the guilt and shame that it felt.

It wasn't that I didn't love Donovan, because I did. However, over the past six months things had changed for me. In addition to my already busy schedule as a third year medical student, I had started to become more active in my church, Berean Christian Church in Stone Mountain. Pastor Lee was one anointed man of God and his wife was amazing.

Ironically, church was how I met Donovan three years ago. I was visiting churches with my best friend and fellow sorority sister, Rochelle. We had both moved from Texas to Georgia to attend professional school. I had just been accepted to Morehouse School of Medicine's medical program and she was accepted to Clark Atlanta University's MBA program.

It was during service when I met Donovan. He was sitting behind me and Pastor Lee was having the congregation give massages to their "cousins" in front of them and behind them. I remember thinking his hands felt amazing and thanking God for the brief stress reliever. And then it was my turn to return the favor. I turned around and was face to face with the finest specimen I had seen in a long time. Not since my first love, Rashad, and he was fine! But Dee was absolutely gorgeous. His hazel eyes complimented his caramel skin tone and he had a smile that made my heart melt. I returned his smile and thought, "God, please do not let him be gay or down low."

Instead of giving him a massage, I turned back around to face the pulpit and focused on keeping my hormones in check. After church he went out of his way to stop me. He was at least six feet tall and he seemed far from gay. We exchanged numbers that day and the rest was history.

I wish someone would have thrown a flag on the play like they do in football games. Don't get me wrong, Dee is a great person and he will make an awesome husband one day, but he came with a little bit of baggage. Now I know we all have baggage, but he didn't share with me in the first few dates that he had a ghetto pregnant ex-girlfriend named Sheba Watkins. Nope! He left that part out of the story.

I didn't find out until two months after we started dating when she gave birth to his now three-year-old son, Justice. I even had to drag it out of him because he went M.I.A. for two days and finally confessed. I don't know why I gave him another chance. I knew that I didn't need that type of drama in my life. I had enough on my plate with medical school. However, the sex was amazing and I didn't want my numbers to go up. He was the third man that I had slept with since Rashad ended our relationship during our junior year of undergrad.

Once I finished showering and getting dressed, I went into the living room of Dee's apartment. He was already in the kitchen cooking dinner for us. That was one thing I loved about Dee. He could cook his tail off!

"Mmm. Smells good babe," I said as I sat down on the couch to read the latest issue of Essence magazine.

"Just a little something special for my lady," he responded.

"Well, it smells delicious, baby. It smells like my favorite pasta dish," I said in a sing song voice.

"It might be." I heard the smile in his voice.

Fifteen minutes later, we were sitting at the dining room table eating chicken alfredo, arugula salad, and garlic bread sticks.

Dee tried to be hood but he was far from it. The things he rapped about made it seem like he was "about that life," but he really came from a great middle class family. His father passed away when he was 16 from prostate cancer and his mother moved him and sister down to Atlanta from Baltimore to be closer to her family.

"So, I've been thinking about some things babe," Dee started as he finished his plate. I already knew where he was going and I didn't know how I was going to turn him down gently.

"What have you been thinking, Dee?" I asked with a hint of attitude.

"Why you already got an attitude and I ain't even asked you anything?"

"You're right. I'm sorry. Go ahead, love."

He looked at me with hesitation because he knew I knew what he wanted to ask.

"I just think we should move in together and I don't see why we don't make that move."

Now it was my turn to look at him before responding. I think I sat there too long because he started to get up to clear the table.

"Wait," I said, grabbing his hand and motioning with my head for him to sit. I took a deep breath and closed my eyes before I responded to him.

"I love you, Dee and I want nothing more than to be with you. However, I'm not moving in with you unless we're married."

"Brooke, I hear ya, but you're always over here and all your shh... I mean your stuff is here. Well, most of it is anyways."

"I know, Dee. Let me get through this next year of med school and we can revisit this topic. Tonight I just want to catch my Sunday night shows and-"

I was interrupted by a loud knock on the door. I felt my body tense up as I looked Dee straight in the eyes. He moved his eyes away from mine and started to get up to answer the door.

"She doesn't call before she comes over!" I spat at him as he opened the door.

"No trick, I don't. I come whenever the hell I want to," Sheba spat back at me.

Sheba Watkins, the ghetto baby mama from hell, waltzed in with poor Justice in tow. Justice was the spitting image of Dee and looked terrified as he walked in with his mother. Sheba and I have never gotten along given the circumstances of how we found out about each other. Even though she was ghetto, she was pretty with dark brown eyes and flawless brown skin. We were about the same height but she weighed at least 20 pounds more than me. She was what we black folks considered thick. Her weaves were always immaculate and she dressed in the latest fashion, which probably came from her dope dealing boyfriend.

She disgusted me. She only used Dee when she wanted to go out or when she needed more money. Thankfully, she did make sure Justice looked presentable and never tacky.

"Justice, go put your stuff in your room," Dee said without acknowledging the tension that was building.

"Why is this hoe always over here? I mean damn, don't she got a home or sumthin?" she asked Dee as if I wasn't present.

I didn't say anything at first because I wanted to see if Dee would stand up for me. That was a problem we had when it came to dealing with Sheba. For some reason, he got mute when the two of us were in the same room.

When he took too long to respond to her, I got up from the dining room table and started to walk to Dee's room to grab my purse and keys. I didn't get out of earshot before I heard her start back up again. I couldn't help myself. I had to say something to her.

"Let me be clear with you, Sheba. I'm not the one you want to go there with. For the past three years, you've been running your mouth. The only reason I haven't whipped your ass is because, unlike you, I have too much to lose. I'm here and I'm not going anywhere. So, I suggest you keep my name out of your mouth!"

"Oh, for real Brooke!? What you trying to do bit- " she started to fire back but Dee gave her a look that let her know to back down.

I kept on walking to the room. By the time I got back to the living room she had already left. Dee reached out to grab my hand, but I moved back. There was silence between us as we just looked at each other. His eyes pleaded with me not to go, but he could tell that I was going home tonight.

"Tell Justice I said sorry," I told Dee as I walked past him and out the door. When I got inside of my car I started to cry because I really needed to figure this relationship out. I wiped my eyes and looked in the rearview mirror. "Girl, you are in med school. What the heck is your problem?" I asked myself.

As I was looking up in my mirror, I could see Dee running down his stairs and making his way over to my car. I quickly pulled myself together and started up my car. For a split second I thought about running him over. I guess he could read my mind because his steps slowed before reaching my car.

He motioned with his hands for me to roll my window down. I shot him the bird. I knew it was petty but I didn't care at the moment. He motioned again and this time I rolled down the passenger side window. I figure that would give me enough distance from him and him an opportunity not to get his foot ran over if I needed to make a quick pull off.

"What?!" I spat.

"Babe, I'm sorry. Please don't leave like this."

"I cannot do this with you, Dee. I mean this some straight ghetto foolishness."

"I love you, B. I told her that she was out of line and that she-"

"Oh, so you do possess a pair of balls? You mean to tell me that you actually stood up for me? Hell must be about to freeze over," I said, cutting him off.

I knew it was a low blow and that I was wrong but I didn't care. At this point, I was fuming with him. Dee has always been passive. I knew it stemmed from his need to please everyone, especially his mother. He took on the heavy burden of being the man of the house once his dad died. However, his mother had a hard time telling the difference between the fact that he was her son and not her man. I was not his mother's number one fan.

I continued, "Don't look so crazy. You know good and well you don't ever stand up for me. You constantly allow her and your crazy mama to disrespect me. I am so tired, man."

I jumped when he slammed his large hands on the roof of my car. He kept his hands there and leaned over to where I couldn't see his face. When he lifted his face up, his hazel eyes were wet and his face had turned red. In the three years we've dated, I've never seen this much emotion from him. We stared at each other as if in a western showdown. He moved first by clearing his throat.

"What are you trying to say Brooke?" his voice barely above a whisper.

I breathed deeply before slowly informing him, "I need time, Donovan."

"Time to do what?"

"To re-evaluate this relationship."

"Brooke, babe, I love you so much. I promise you that I won't ever let her or my mother disrespect you again. You have my word and you know I keep my word."

He reached through the window and extended his pinky finger inches from where my right arm lay on the arm rest. I looked at his pinky and then at his eyes. I searched them for deception but I couldn't see any. I extended and wrapped my pinky around his.

I sighed and asked, "Pinky promise?"

"You got my word. Now, will you come back upstairs?"

Once back inside, I was greeted by Justice, who obviously must have been watching his father and I through the blinds. They were stuck open and the footstool was by the window.

"Ms. Brooke are you going to stay and make the cookies for me tonight?"

I patted him on his head and smiled.

"Of course I am, sweetie."

Chapter 2

Rashad

"Mooooom," I moaned with annoyance.

At least what I hoped to sound like annoyance and not pleasure. I was on the phone with my mother, but she kept on talking as if she didn't hear me. I looked down at Victoria, who wasn't my current girlfriend, in the process of giving me the best head ever. She looked up at me and smiled while still holding me in her mouth. She then held up one of her manicured hands and gave me the 'keep talking' gesture. She went back to work and I was having a hard time concentrating on what my mother was talking about.

"Boy, do you hear me?" my mother snapped.

"I wish I didn't," I thought. However, I responded, "Yes, ma'am."

I could hear my mother shuffling some papers in the background at her law office. She's a law partner at one the largest law firms in Dallas and is the reason I decided to pursue a career as an attorney. After I graduated from UGA I opted not to head back to Texas for law school and got accepted into Emory's law program. I was counting down the days until my graduation at the end of the upcoming fall semester. Nonetheless, I admired my mother. She never sacrificed her family for her career. I cannot remember her missing any of my football games or my younger brother's basketball games. She also managed not to miss my father's sermons on Sunday. She was definitely a super woman and I hoped to marry a woman half as amazing as my mother.

"Well, are you going to call him, Shad? It is his birthday," my mother said. I could hear the plea in her tone.

The him she was referring to was my father. My father and I had a strained relationship ever since I could remember. It became worse once I entered into high school and if it weren't for my mother, I'm not sure where I would have ended up.

When I left Texas to play ball at UGA, I left his 'holier than thou' lifestyle and got a chance to experience life on my own terms. I knew God, but the way my father presented Him to me turned me off from religion. He expected a lot from me as the oldest and most times it was overbearing.

He was so heavenly bound that he was no earthly good. He tried to control my mother, but she was too independent. I am still trying to figure out how they have been married for 25 years.

"Yes, I will call him, but Mom I gotta- ouch," I said as looked down at Victoria. It felt like she scrapped me with her teeth, which I thought would be hard to do considering the gap between her two front teeth. I gave her a sharp look and she peered up at me with smile, still holding me in her mouth.

"Son, you alright over there?" my mother asked with a hint of sarcasm.

"Yes, ma'am. Just stubbed my toe," I lied.

"Stubbed your toe? Hmm… okay."

I could tell my mother knew that I was lying and I wasn't in a position to convince her otherwise. I was ready to get off the phone with her before I couldn't control any more of my outbursts.

"Son, I worry about you with those young ladies down in Atlanta. I know you think I'm just being an overprotective mother, and maybe I am, but I only want what's best for you. I love you, Shad," she said.

"I love you, too, Mom."

"I wish you would have worked things out with Brooke. She is so sweet and really loved you for you and not for your pedigree."

At the mention of Brooke's name my dick deflated and there was no point of return. I hated when Mom mentioned her name. Hell, I hated the fact that my family was still close with hers. It was a constant reminder of my biggest failure. I knew I had let an incredible woman go because I was selfish, in addition to being young, dumb and full of cum.

I ended my relationship with Brooke the summer going into my junior year. There was a lot of power that came with being on the football team and it didn't help that I was one of the starting wide receivers. I had grown women and their daughters throwing their panties at me and I could no longer resist temptation. I wanted to live life on my own terms and Brooke was a hindrance at that time in my life. Plus the long distance was not working for me. I had needs that could not wait for the scheduled school breaks.

Instead of cheating on her, I ended the relationship via Skype. I spared her the real reason why I was breaking up with her, telling her some bull about having to focus on my school work. Knowing damn well I had one of my many groupies doing my work. I will never forget the pain in her eyes and the sound of her cry. She sounded like a wounded animal. She wiped her eyes and looked straight into her webcam. I would have died a slow death if the look she gave me could kill.

Brooke cleared her throat before she spoke. "You know, Rashad," she said with a measured calmness. "I love you so much. I've loved you since we were kids playing in the sandbox, but I don't believe a damn thing you just said to me. You are more like your father than you think you are."

With that statement she disconnected the call and that was the last time we spoke to each other. She must have immediately deleted me from all of her social networking sites because when I went to search for her name it never came up. I tried reaching out to her for at least six months after the break-up. I at least wanted us to be friends. However, she never answered any of my calls or responded to any of my texts or emails. If it wasn't for my mother or my brother, I wouldn't know if she was alive.

"I know, Mom. I messed that one up."

By this time, Victoria was standing up and was visibly pissed. I could tell she heard my mother's last statement about Brooke and my response didn't help. I mouthed to her 'sorry' and gave her the 'I'll call you later' sign. She gave me the finger, grabbed her belongings, and was out the door. I knew I wouldn't call her and planned to avoid her like the plague at school.

Brooke was my first and only love. Not even my current girlfriend, Natalie, compared to her. I tried to love Natalie on the level that I loved Brooke, but I couldn't. I can't put my finger on it. She was clingy at times, but tried to appear independent. In subtle ways she attempted to control who I hung around. I knew the game and I knew how to keep a woman happy. Happy enough to do me and other women like Victoria.

I got up off my couch and locked the door behind Victoria, who had been kind enough to slam the door on her way out of my apartment. I continued talking to my mother for few more minutes and then got off the phone with her to prepare for my class later that evening. I debated calling my father but decided I would wait until my day was over. I needed to be on my way to sleep before I could entertain any conversation with him.

"You can't be serious, Rashad? The court's decision in this case was completely erroneous," one of my classmates said to me after our health care law class.

I chuckled, "James, I hate to admit this to you, but your boy Scalia got it right this time. It's not often that happens, but in this case he did."

I could tell James was becoming ruffled by his olive skin darkening with emotion. He rubbed his left hand through his black hair and gave me a doubtful look with his green eyes. These types of conversations were not new to us. It had been like this since the first day we met in law school. He quickly became like another brother to me. The only difference was that he was Italian.

Before James could respond, his attention went to whatever was behind me. I turned around to see what had his attention and was warmly greeted by my girl, Natalie.

"Hey baby," she said with a kiss to my cheek.

She turned her tall body into mine and wrapped her slender arm through mine. She then focused her attention on James. He obviously got the hint because he reached out to dap me up.

"Alright man," he said. "I'll catch you later. Don't forget we have practice tomorrow evening."

"Yeah, I will be there, bruh."

James walked off without speaking to Natalie. Natalie and James didn't care for each other. James felt as if Natalie was one step from being locked up in an asylum. I didn't think she was that bad, but she definitely displayed questionable tendencies. She didn't like me to talking to other women and always wanted to be around me, but what woman didn't do that?

She was no different than other girls I've dated. I'm a good looking guy who comes from a good family, no criminal record, and no baby mama drama. I knew I was a rare find these days. She also attempted to control who I hung out with and James was one person she felt I could do without in my life. So I kept the two of them separate from each other.

"I don't know why you talk to him still. Especially after I told you how he tried to hit on me at my 1L mixer a few weeks ago," she said as we begin to walk outside to the parking deck.

I ignored her statement and asked her if she was still coming to my apartment tonight. She nodded her oval head in the affirmative. Natalie was a beautiful third generation Ethiopian with silky, shoulder length jet black hair. She had smooth brown skin and most people mistook her for Indian descent. Her dark brown eyes were big and round and always told how she was feeling.

As we walked towards her car, an older model Lexus was backing out of the stall next to hers. I knew the car and the driver very well and I began to get hotter than a pair of monkey balls in the rain forest. The driver rolled down her tinted window and gave a warm sparkling smile to both Natalie and I.

"Hey Tori!" Natalie said, excitedly, "I haven't seen you since you left this morning, roomie."

Natalie let go of my hand to reach in and hug Tori, aka Victoria. The same Victoria who was giving me one of the best blow jobs earlier that day at my place.

Victoria pushed her D&G designer frames back up her nose as their embrace ended. She gave me a quick sideways glance before responding back to Natalie.

"Girl, you know I had my kickboxing class this morning. It's starting to suck because it's getting so hard. The instructor is such a dickhead, but he's so fine. You should come though," Victoria said with a smirk.

"You right girl. I'm going to go with you next time," Natalie responded naively.

"You should come. I'm sure the instructor could teach you a few things. Plus you could learn how to best protect yourself from these crazies out here."

"Girl, who needs protection when I got this strong black man looking out for me?"

Victoria laughed before saying, "I bet Shad is very good protection to have."

I chuckled in my head at the exchange. Victoria knew how to stay in her lane regarding our situation. I guess she wasn't as mad as I thought she was. Victoria was in her second year of law school and I started messing around with her during her first year. I kept her on the team because of her immaculate head game. It probably was the gap in her teeth that kept me coming back. It wasn't a big gap, but it was enough that when she pulled me just right I was guaranteed to be a happy man.

Victoria was also cool to kick it with. We hung out plenty of times without smashing. She was good people but I knew she wasn't someone I wanted to settle down with. Something about giving up the draws on the first night is a major turn off for me.

I began to look at my watch. It was getting late and I still needed to call my father. I had to wrap this conversation up before Victoria accidentally let something slip out.

"Babe, you still coming over to the house right?" I asked Natalie.

"Yes, silly. Let me get in the car now so I can follow you over," she said walking away with a wave to Victoria.

"Don't wait up for me, girl. I'm going to stay over with Shad," she said over the roof of her car.

"Ya'll just make sure you wrap it up. I'd hate for you to catch anything," Victoria said with a laugh as she pulled out.

"Honey, Shad know I would kill him if he did anything crazy like that," Natalie said laughing as she got in the car.

"Bye Shad!" Victoria yelled out and threw her hand out the window to wave. I didn't even attempt to wave or speak.

By the time Natalie and I made it back to my place it was already close to ten my time, which meant it was almost nine in Texas. We made a stop to grab something to eat before heading to my apartment and ended up talking for a while at the restaurant.

Our conversations were always great. I often felt guilty that I couldn't love her, or even treat her, the way she deserved to be treated. Tonight was one of those nights. However, I had to get over that guilt and prepare my mind for the potential war with my father. I knew he was going to trip out that I was calling him so late. Hell, he should be glad I'm calling him at all. If I didn't promise my mother that I would call him I definitely wouldn't waste my free minutes.

"Babe, I'm going to jump in the shower. I'm so tired from the day," Natalie said walking toward the bathroom in my bedroom.

"That's cool, love. I got to call my dad anyways. It's his birthday."

"Well, tell the great reverend I said happy birthday."

"Sure will, babe."

I pulled my phone out of my pocket and sat down on my couch in the living room. I stared at my plain beige walls for a moment, trying to think of excuses to tell my mother as to why I didn't call my father. I couldn't think of any great ones so I made the call. I almost hung up but he decided to pick up on what seemed like the fourth ring.

"Boy, do you know what time it is?" he spat angrily.

I could see his big nostrils flaring up and his beady eyes squinting as he spoke to me with venom. I closed my eyes, breathed deeply, and said a quick prayer for strength before I responded.

"Yes sir, I do," was all I could manage respectfully.

"Well, what the hell do you want? I have to get up early to preach at a youth revival."

You would never know my father was a man of the cloth with the language he used. In fact, he was the pastor of one of the largest Church of God in Christ, or COGIC for short, churches in the Dallas area.

My grandfather was the pastor of Destiny New Life COGIC until it was time for him to retire from the pulpit. My father was next in line to pastor the congregation and couldn't wait to jump on the opportunity. He was a new school preacher and was able to grow the church from 500 faithfuls to at least 5,000 within a five year span.

He managed to get a deal to get the church on television and stream all the worship services live online. It's amazing

what he has accomplished in a short period of time. I swear
he had already planned his takeover from the time he was a
boy. The people in the community thought my father was a
saint and really lived the life he preached about, but I could
see through his deceit because at home he was a different
man.

"I called to tell you happy birthday," I said calmly. I felt
a tension headache coming on so I got up to pour myself a
shot of tequila.

"The day is damn near over, I mean seriously son why
did you call? You couldn't have wanted to wish me a happy
birthday. Not at nine o'clock at night."

Again, I breathed deeply and prayed before responding.

"Sir, I did call to wish you a happy birthday. I had
classes today and this is the first I've had time to call you."

"Bullshit boy!" he cackled on the other end. "You mean
to tell me that you had classes all day? Ain't you in summer
school?"

"I'm also on the mock trial team and we're preparing
for a competition, so my day was full," I said with little
more force than I should have.

I heard my father clear his throat. I knew I crossed the
line with my tone but I didn't care. I was growing tired of
the bullshit and I had moved my finger to the talk button on
my Bluetooth, ready to end the call.

"You have yourself a goodnight," he said, dryly.

Before I could respond, he disconnected the other line.
A single tear fell from my eye but before any more could
fall, I made myself another shot and headed to my
bedroom.

As I walked closer to my bedroom I could hear the shower water running. I knew that after that conversation, or the lack thereof, I had to release my raging emotions. I quickly stripped my clothes off and let them hit the bedroom floor. I wanted to make sure I could still catch Natalie nice and wet.

Chapter 3

Brooke

"Ma'am, you did not call and say you were going to be late. Thus per office policy, we are going to have to charge you a $25 cancellation fee," I said to the increasingly irate patient standing behind the counter at the doctor's office.

I was at my part-time job where I was an assistant for a family friend, Dr. Patrice Neal, at her ob/gyn practice. Usually, I was working rounds with her or helping out in the clinic, but once a week I had the pleasure of working the front office. It wasn't that bad, but there was always that one patient who potentially needed to see a psychiatrist and not a gynecologist. This was that patient.

"How are you gonna tell me I ain't call you?" she yelled at me while flipping her platinum blonde weave from her right shoulder to her left.

Let me tell you, God made us in all beautiful shades of brown but platinum blonde hair is not sexy on a midnight black sista, nor was the hot pink leather looking mini skirt with a neon yellow halter top a good look on her. Looking at her made me want to grab a bag of Skittles and taste the rainbow. However, I praised Jesus that she covered up her triple D breasts with some sort of fabric, that I am sure at one point was a cardigan. Let me not even get started on her long, cat-like nails similar to length and style like Coko from SWV. They had the nerve to be painted pink and green.

I closed my eyes and took a deep breath before I gently spoke to her. "Ma'am, I'm going to need you to calm down. If you give me a moment I can look in the system again and-"

"Trick! I want to see your manager. You ain't even the damn doctor. You just a secretary!"

Before I could reach over the counter to slap Miss Hood Booger, Dr. Neal came running to the front of the office. I assume one of the nurses called her to tell her of the fire that was brewing in her respectable practice. Thankfully there was only one other patient in the waiting area and a couple of patients in the examination rooms.

"Miss Wilcox," Dr. Neal said, raising her hand, shaking her head side to side, while trying to catch her breath. "Please come with me to my office so we can talk."

I don't know what happened, but Miss Hood Booger became sweet as pie. I couldn't believe that this was the same women that wanted to rip my head off because she did not understand the concept of time. She didn't say another word to me and proceeded to walk with Dr. Neal to her office. However, Dr. Neal stopped her by putting her hand up and looked over at me.

"Miss Wilcox, before we go discuss your visit today, I am going to need you to apologize to Dr. Jones. I do not appreciate the language or tone that was used with my colleague and I hope that this is not how you speak to any of my other staff," Dr. Neal said with a stern, yet gentle tone.

It took everything in me not to laugh as Miss Wilcox sheepishly apologized. I didn't say anything but just nodded my head with a smirk.

The rest of the day went by smoothly after that fiasco with Miss Wilcox. Unfortunately for her, the appointment was rescheduled for another day that she felt confident she could be on time for and for further punishment, she had to pay the $25 cancellation fee.

"I don't know how you do it, Patrice," I said with a sigh as I sat down in the oversized leather chair in her office.

"Girl, with a glass of wine and lots of prayer," she said as she sat behind her desk.

Patrice reached in one of her drawers and pulled out a little bottle of wine. I laughed as I took the bottle and put it in my purse.

"I can use this for later on," I said.

She smiled and leaned back in her chair. I could tell she had a lot on her mind and that she was getting ready to unload something heavy on me. I had known Patrice since I was 18. Our mothers worked together before my mother moved into administration within our school district back in Dallas. At the time Patrice and I met, she was getting ready to graduate from Baylor with her bachelor's degree. We hit it off instantly and kept in touch when she went away to medical school.

"I'm pregnant, Brooke," she said with solemnness. The way she said it was more like a death sentence than the blessing that children are supposed to be.

"I'm pregnant and I don't know if I want to keep my baby," she continued.

I didn't say anything because I didn't know what to say to her at that moment. I was excited for her because I knew she wanted to have children. At the same time, I was confused by her tone regarding this wonderful news. At least I thought it was wonderful news. All I could manage to ask her was why she felt the way she did.

Patrice began to cry. At first it was a silent cry, but it quickly became a violent one. I was glad that we were the only two left in the office. I could only imagine what her employees or her patients would think of her if they saw her crying the way that she was. They would probably be more shocked at her statement about not wanting to keep her child.

"Brooke, I love Quentin and all, but he grabbed me the other day. I'm not sure I want to have a child with a person who is capable of harming me. I haven't told him that I'm pregnant because it is still pretty early. I'm trying to get out of this marriage with my life and I do not want a child to suffer because their father is a monster."

I felt my face scrunch up and my eyebrows raise but again I said nothing. Her marriage was one to envy, at least from the outside looking in. Her husband, Quentin, was an amazing man who would do anything to keep her happy. Something told me that there was more to this story because it didn't make sense as to why he would ever lay a hand on her.

"Trice, whatever you want to do, I'm here for you. I'm at a loss of words. Like, how did this happen?"

"He lost his job about a month ago and didn't tell me. I found out because I came home early and he was there. I asked him why he was home so early and he just went in defense mode."

I sat and waited a few moments for her to continue with her story, but when she didn't say anything else I realized that was it. By now her tears had dried up and she had appeared to have calmed herself down. I'm guessing her pregnancy hormones had mellowed out for a brief moment. However, her story didn't jive with me. I still couldn't imagine Quentin placing his hands on her.

I've seen how she has treated men in the past. Let's just say she is a witch who wears Louboutins. Poor Quentin was a brave soul to put a ring on her finger. She was a mean little something and had a very ugly way of belittling men. Hell, it was amazing she had any friends, let alone a husband, because she's just a mean spirited person.

The only time she knew how to be nice was when things were going her way and she was in control of things. She took being spoiled to a whole different level. Maybe that was because she was an only child and didn't have to share her toys with anyone.

She and I got into it one time while I was attending undergrad. Matter of fact, we were arguing about my break up with Rashad and I had to let her know that she wasn't the only one who could get crazy. Once she discovered that I hadn't always had a relationship with Jesus, we never had any more issues again.

"Trice, I feel like you are leaving a lot out of your story. I'm not sure why you are either because I know you. I have known you for over ten years and you are like a big sister to me. So please don't forget I've seen how you can get down with men. I'm sure there are plenty of brothers who wanted to smack the mess out of you. I've wanted to haul off and smack you myself a few times. You're the true epitome of the devil wears Prada! So, let's try this story again and this time I would like the uncut version please."

She chuckled before saying, "You really do know me, don't you?"

I smiled and nodded.

"Well," she sighed, "The first part of the story is true. I did come home early and found him at home. It's also true that he lost his job last month. He had known that he was going to lose his job about six months prior due the company downsizing. He's been looking since he found out about what they were doing. I remember him saying something to the effect that he was going to start looking for a new opportunity or even start his own consulting firm. I blew it off.

Anyway, the argument escalated and I slapped him in his face. I can't even remember what he said that made me slap him. Probably nothing rude, but I was pissed. I do remember telling him that he was a sorry MF and that he had better find employment by the end of the month. He grabbed me and pushed me up against the wall but that was after I slapped him for the second time.

When he did that, I spat in his face. Brooke, the look he gave me was one of death. He let me go and within an hour he had packed up some of his clothes and left. He hasn't been home for a week now and he doesn't know I'm pregnant. That, my sweet sister, is the truth."

I sat there stunned by the information she shared with me. I couldn't believe this beautiful and intelligent black woman was this crazy.

"You need to get help, Trice. Why do you allow yourself to go there? You're so spoiled and for whatever reason you think that the sun rises and sets on your command. If I were Quentin, I would have slapped the remaining saliva out of your mouth before I packed my stuff to leave your behind."

Patrice looked at me with her sad, big brown eyes. Her eyes misted up but she didn't let a tear fall. Instead, she sighed and reached her slender hands across her desk for mine. I gave her my hand and for a few moments we shared a few unspoken words.

"I love you, Brooke," she said with a smile. "You're the only person who I know that is able to read me and not even show a hint of intimidation."

"Girl, I love you so much but you have to be reminded that when God made you it was not to be Jesus Jr.," I said laughing.

We shared a few more laughs together and worked out a plan to win her husband back. The first step being to apologize, followed by intensive therapy.

Later that evening, I was getting ready to hang out with Rochelle and her cousin, Natalie. I didn't know why Rochelle insisted on bringing Natalie around. She knew how much I couldn't stand her cousin. She knew as well as

I did that her cousin was psycho, but it was her family. So I played nice with Natalie when she came around for the sake of my friendship with Rochelle.

As I was slipping on my shoes I got a video call from my middle sister, Breanne.

"Hey Bree. What's new with you girl? I am loving the hair color! Who knew that auburn would look so nice on you," I said with a chuckle.

My sister feigned a look of offense as she shook her shoulder length hair side to side.

"Girl, you know I look good and don't you even try to deny all of this sexy!" she said followed by her infamous Count Dracula laugh.

"Oh Bree, please don't do that laugh!"

"I can't help it. I've been trying to find new ways to change my laugh up, but I can't. Parker says he finds my laugh infectious."

I smiled and rolled my eyes playfully at my sister. Although, Breanne was three years younger than me, there was no denying that she was my sister. She and I shared the same mocha skin complexion, the same eye shape and color, and both of our bodies were built like the famous coke bottle.

"How are you and Parker doing? Is he planning on coming down with you for the Greek picnic next weekend?" I asked her while putting on last minute make-up and accessories.

"Uh huh. We're going to drive down on Thursday when he gets off work. I should have told him that I was flying because that is a long ass drive from Dallas to Atlanta."

"Don't I know it? Hence why I asked was he still coming. I thought for sure you would have flown down."

"I wanted to but I knew how much Parker wanted to go see his brother. Speaking of his brother..." there was a hesitation in her voice before saying, "You know he wants us to stay with him."

I looked down at my phone, which I had propped up against my bathroom sink. I didn't say anything to her, I just stared at her as if she had grown two heads. I wasn't sure if I felt betrayed, angry, or hurt by her comment. Either way I had a hard time believing that my sister would even consider staying with Rashad, Parker's brother.

I could understand Parker staying with his brother, but not my sister staying with the enemy. After all of these years, I still hadn't forgiven him. I made it very clear to my family that I didn't want to know anything about Rashad's life.

"If that black negro was eaten by a bunch of angry piranhas, please don't invite me to his funeral," were my exact words to my family. Bree did, however, share with me that he moved back to Atlanta to attend law school after I got accepted at Morehouse School of Medicine. She never told me what school he had been accepted to because I changed the subject and she never brought it back up again.

My worst fear was running into him on the streets of Atlanta and seeing him happy with someone else. Thankfully, my prayers to not see him have been working for the past three years.

"Brooke," my sister said, remorsefully. I didn't say anything but I acknowledged her by looking directly into the screen. "I was never going to stay with him. I told Parker I was going to be staying with you and that I would meet him where ever. However, we decided it would be best if we stayed in a hotel room. That way nobody will feel uncomfortable."

I still didn't say anything to her but I breathed out a sigh of relief. We were silent for a moment. I knew that my sister felt bad about the information she shared with me but I wasn't mad at her and I needed to let her know that.

"Bree, I love you and I appreciate you for telling me what was going on. I think I need to pray a little harder. I still cannot stand him. You didn't even mention his name and I become so enraged on the inside. I think my life would be better if you didn't date Parker," I said with laugh.

She laughed too and rolled her eyes at me.

"Well, Parker is here to stay honey. It would have been nice for us to have our double wedding, but that is a distant fantasy of mine. By the way, you look super pretty! Your boobs are huge! Did you let one of your plastic surgeon friends experiment on your titties?" she cackled.

I shook my head and laughed. Leave it to my sister to point out my growing body parts. I didn't answer her because I had a feeling I knew why my boobs were growing all of sudden. If the God I served was as merciful and kind as I believed him to be, then what I was thinking would be wrong.

"Whatever girl, I gotta go. I'm hanging with Rochelle and her crazy cousin," I said, avoiding her statement about my breasts.

"Well, have fun chick! I love you, boop."

"I love you, too, boop."

"Girl, this spot is so whack. Let's go next door to eat. I'm hungry!" Rochelle shouted over the loud music. She even exaggerated her hunger by rubbing her stomach.

I nodded my head because I was hungry too, but I was more tired than hungry.

"Where is Natalie?" I asked as we started walking towards the door.

Rochelle craned her long neck to see over the crowd which wasn't hard for her to do because she is almost six foot without her heels.

"Hmm…I don't know. Let me text her and let her know we are going outside," she said as she pulled out her phone to text her cousin.

While we waited for Natalie to come outside, I shared with Rochelle my conversation with my sister.

"I mean it has been at least four or five years now since we've broken up. For the most part my family does a great job of not mentioning his name around me. I know that has to be hard on Bree because she is dating his brother. Shoot, if it wasn't for her I wouldn't have known that he moved back to Georgia to go to law school. She never told me what school he got accepted to because I told her I didn't want to know. I'm pitiful, huh?"

Rochelle shook her head. "Brooke, you're going to have let that hurt go," she said. "You have to remember that forgiveness is not an option. We don't get to decide if we're going to forgive or not. God forgives with no questions asked. Just because you forgive doesn't mean you won't still hurt or even be angry, but forgiveness allows us to move forward in the healing process. You have moved on and I'm sure he has too."

I crossed my arms in front of my chest and lowered my head as I allowed the truth of her words to sink in my spirit. I knew that I had to forgive him. It wasn't fair for me to make my family tiptoe around me when it concerned him.

As I was battling with forgiving Rashad, Natalie's loud behind came out of the club.

"Hey ya'll! I'm sorry. The line in the bathroom was crazy. I ran into this cutie, so I got caught up flirting," she practically yelled at us.

I rolled my eyes in disgust at her. She really got under my skin. Everything about her screamed crazy! I couldn't put my finger on what exactly it was about her, but I knew something about her wasn't right.

"Nat," Rochelle said, "We're outside now boo, you don't have to yell. Also, don't you have a man? You shouldn't even be entertaining these fools out here."

It was Natalie's turn to roll her eyes. Instead of answering her cousin's question, she started walking toward the direction of where we parked at.

"I guess she told you," I whispered in Rochelle's ear as we walked behind Natalie.

"She gets on my darn nerves. She was just telling me how much she loves Shad. Mind you, they have only been dating since the semester started. They haven't been together long enough to be in love."

"Please don't start worrying yourself about other people's problems. She's grown. Maybe she was trying to get a drink or something before you text. What we really need to discuss is what we're going to eat because your girl is hungry!"

As we walked to Rochelle's car, I wondered if Shad was short for Rashad. What were the chances that Natalie could be dating *my* Rashad? I shook my head and quickly dismissed that thought. His name was a dime a dozen. God wouldn't be that cruel to allow Rashad to be dating someone in my circle, even if that person wasn't necessarily my friend. Would He?

Chapter 4

Brooke

I was hot, naked and alone in my bed, but not alone in my house. I could smell turkey bacon frying and hear dishes moving around in my kitchen. Dee always got up before me on the weekends to make me breakfast. I had texted him last night before we left the burger restaurant we crashed after leaving that whack club. He was at the studio working but he managed to still beat me to my apartment.

When I walked into my apartment, I noticed that he washed the dishes that I left in the sink and had straightened up the place. As I was walking past my dining room table to head to the bedroom, I had noticed he left a card on the table and a bag of Skittles for me.

"I guess I will get to taste the rainbow after all." I remembered chuckling to myself as read the card.

It was moments like that which reminded me of why I loved him and wanted to make our relationship work. He never came to my house empty handed. He always had some small gift for me. I never had to ask him to restock my fridge. If he finished something, he always replaced it. His mother taught him well. He was a good man, but I knew in my heart he was not the one. I kept thinking that if

I gave him some more time to grow he would eventually become the man I needed him to be.

Before I got out of the bed, I reached over to my nightstand to check my cell phone. I saw I had a text message from my mother reminding me that her and my father would be flying in later that evening and staying until Wednesday for my father's conference. I crinkled my face up and cussed in my head because I had forgotten they were coming into town. I quickly got up out of the bed and put on my robe. As I opened my room door to walk across to my bathroom, I ran smack into Dee's chest.

"Good morning, sweets," he said bending down to give me a kiss on my forehead.

I smiled as I looked up at him to return the kiss he gave me on my forehead, but then I smelled something that sent my stomach into a frenzy! I quickly pushed past him and made it to the toilet in time to release my stomach contents from last night.

Dee came running in behind me and immediately turned on the shower for me and helped me off the floor. Except my stomach was not done with me yet, so back to the toilet I went. This time I was dry heaving for a few seconds, but it felt like an eternity.

"Are you okay, babe?" he asked, worriedly.

I could only nod my head as I moved past him to get in the shower. I didn't drink anything at the club. I didn't even have a chance to open the mini wine bottle Patrice had given me. I stood in the shower trying to ponder what the heck was going on with my body. My period was due any day now. I was only a few days late. Well, maybe a week late, but my period did weird things from time to time. I closed my eyes as I let the water run freely over my body.

"Dang, am I?" I asked aloud to myself.

"What is it, babe? Did you drink too much last night? Or maybe you're pregnant. Wouldn't that be cool," he said, hopeful.

"Oh my gosh! You're still in here!"

"Sitting right here on the toilet," he laughed. "I ran out the bathroom to turn off the food so it wouldn't burn up, but I wanted to make sure you were okay. Plus I needed to make sure you weren't going crazy in here talking to yourself."

"No, I'm fine. I'm not pregnant. Probably something I ate last night. You know I don't really drink like that when I'm out," I said as convincingly as I could.

I heard him get up and walk over to the shower. He pulled the shower curtain back enough to poke his head in. I had already started to wash myself and turned to see him checking me out. I smiled as I made a thrusting motion with my pelvis. He laughed and gave me an air kiss before walking out the bathroom.

After I had gotten dressed, I went and sat in my living room. The television was turned on to the sports station and they were showing the latest highlights from the basketball playoffs. I had a towel draped around my shoulders as I contemplated what to do with my natural hair. As I was sitting there, Dee set a plate of food down on the coffee table.

"Do you need me to help with anything in the kitchen?" I asked him as I started to section my hair in order to twist it.

"Nah, you're good, babe. The real question is what are you going to do with that head of yours?" he said as he playfully tussled my hair.

I laughed as I tried to smack his hand away from my hair but he was too quick for me. As he headed back to the kitchen I informed him that my parents were arriving in Atlanta later in the day and that they were probably going to want to have dinner with us.

"That's cool, babe. I would have to run back to my place to grab some clothes to wear. You know your dad likes to floss how much he's balling."

"Whatever, Dee. Just be back here to pick me up on time. I need to text my mother back to see what time they're going to be here and whatnot."

I ignored the latter part of his statement because I knew that it would start an argument. Dee and my father got along very well, but I knew that Dee was intimidated by my father. I tried to explain to him that my father has three daughters and he always provided for his little women. He definitely set a high standard when it came to the men I chose to date, but I never expected Dee to be my father.

I knew what Dee had and what he didn't have. He has always been thoughtful. I believe it was how he compensated for not having as much money and for still being in school working towards his associate's degree. However, I did wish he would give up his idea of becoming the next one hit wonder rapper.

"Would you like more water?" the young waitress asked me as she leaned over to pour. I never understood why waiters asked you that question but never let you respond. Lucky for her, I did want more water. So I just nodded my head.

Dee and I were having dinner with my parents at one of Atlanta's five star restaurants. Dee and I had driven from his apartment to meet them in downtown Atlanta. My mother was fussing with my father's shirt collar, to which my father was acting like he was annoyed.

I truly admired my parents. Their marriage gave me hope in love and that marriage could be a blessing. My parents got married not to long after having me and had been married for almost thirty years. They contributed the success of their marriage to their faith in God, praying parents, and having children. My mother used to tell me that there were plenty of times in the beginning of their marriage that she wanted to leave my father in order to explore life as a young woman. My grandmother was very clear with her that she was not raising another child she didn't birth.

My father, from my understanding, was a bit of a handful in the beginning of their marriage. I have never been able to confirm if my father ever stepped out on the marriage, but I knew he loved to party with his frat brothers without my mother. My parents called it growing pains and said that each couple will experience their own version of such pains. "But if you have a willing party and God as your foundation, you can make it work," my father used to share with my sisters and I.

"Dear, I wish you stop messing with me. I'm a grown man who knows how to dress himself," my father said with a laugh.

"Hmph, if you knew how to dress yourself, your collar wouldn't be sticking up in the back," my mother retorted.

My father looked at Dee and me with pleading eyes. We all laughed as the waitress came back with our entrees. As we ate, I took a moment to look at my parents. They were aging so gracefully. They were only in their forties but they could easily get away with early to mid-thirties.

Bree and I shared the same mocha skin complexion as my mother, but my younger sister took my father's beautiful dark chocolate skin complexion. My mother kept her hair cut short and dyed it regularly to keep her gray hairs hidden. My father was a giant of man in comparison to my mother's five foot seven frame. He kept his hair cut low as well, but did not mind the few gray hairs that begin to sprinkle his head and beard.

"So, Brooke how is working for Patrice going for you?" my mother asked.

"Yesterday was very interesting, Mama. You know how these crazies get from time to time. I had only heard about the rumors but yesterday I got to experience my first real life crazy." I shared with my parents how the hood booger cut up in the office and how Dee had unknowingly satisfied my craving for Skittles.

"Oh Brooke, this only the beginning of great things to come," my father said with a laugh. Then he turned serious. "Just think, she's not the only one out there who has that attitude of entitlement. I always tell my new associates to treat everyone with respect. You never know when the janitor is going to become your boss one day."

"That's right sweetie. You two would be wise to remember that and to pray over these people who you come in contact with. You never know what someone is going through," my mother consigned.

"So, Donovan... how are classes going for you son?" my father asked, turning his attention to Dee.

I gave Dee a gentle squeeze under the table as a sign of encouragement. He didn't flinch and kept his focus on my father.

"Well, sir my classes are going well. However, I have been really contemplating joining the Air Force. I think it would be a great way to pay for school and to help take care of my family."

My father's expression lit up at the mention of the Air Force. "That's wonderful, son! My father was an airmen and I was a JAG officer myself. I was able to afford to take care of my young family because of my service to the country. Let me know if..."

My father's words trailed off as I started to choke on my water at this news my boyfriend was sharing with my parents. I was pissed! How could Dee not share this information with me first? He never told me that he was thinking about joining the service.

This was a huge decision to even consider and he was making this announcement to my parents as if we had discussed it already. It wasn't a bad idea for him to join the military because I was pretty sure that his career as a rapper wasn't going to go as far he would like.

"Brooke, are you alright?" my mother asked as she reached over to pat me on the back.

I put my hand up and nodded. "I think I drank my water too fast."

In my peripheral, I saw Dee drinking his water but I could feel his leg shaking. He knew I was searing mad with him and I knew he was nervous as hell about the ride home.

I stayed quiet for most of the remaining dinner with my parents. I could not stop thinking about how Dee didn't share with me his thoughts about the military. It hurt my feelings that he didn't think to tell me something so vital and important to our relationship.

Did he think I wouldn't support his decision to join? I don't know how he would have thought that because I have always carried a soft spot for the military because of my father. I often pondered going in myself but with all that was going in the world I decided against it.

As we waited for the valet to bring our cars, we started to say our goodbyes to my parents. I knew Dee wished that we had driven with my parents to avoid the tongue lashing he was about to get.

"Bye Mama. Thanks for dinner. I hope to see you before you leave so we can go shopping." I winced as we hugged and I tried to fix my face before my mother saw.

"You're welcome baby. You know we're going to visit your church tomorrow and come by. I volunteered to help with conference this year, but I am going to sneak out early on Tuesday. We are leaving early on Wednesday morning, so we will have to do our shopping Tuesday afternoon."

"That's fine because I get off work early on Tuesdays. I usually do clinics in the morning with Patrice."

"Oh and by the way," she said as she leaned into my ear, "I noticed you picked up a little weight. It looks good on you."

"What are you two whispering about?" my father asked, walking up and giving me a hug.

I was so glad that he walked up and saved me from trying to come up with a lie to my mother in regards to my weight gain.

My mother smirked at me."I was letting Brooke know how great she looks."

"You do look great, baby girl. I'm really starting to like Donovan. Maybe one day you two will get married and get us some grandbabies," my father beamed.

I looked over at my mother, who was standing there still smirking at me. I didn't say anything to my father but looked up at him smiling. Dee called out to me when the valet brought his car around. I gave my parents a final hug and kiss before getting in the car with Dee.

We drove in silence for the first fifteen minutes of our ride. I played on my phone and checked my Facebook account. I was stalling trying to figure out how to approach the elephant sitting in the car with us without being confrontational.

"So, when were you going to tell me that you were thinking about going into the Air Force?" I asked as calmly as I could.

At first he didn't say anything but continued to drive as if I hadn't asked him a question. He quickly looked over at me and went back to focusing on the road. I didn't understand why he looked at me and I figured maybe he didn't understand my question.

He sighed. "I've already signed up for the Air Force. I'm leaving in November for basic training."

My head snapped back against the passenger seat. Did I hear this man correctly?

"Say what?" I asked.

"I've been trying to tell you for a minute now. I just didn't know how to without getting you upset."

I still couldn't say anything. It was like the past twenty four hours of my life had been a whirlwind. First the hood booger, followed by Patrice, then this weird stuff with my body, and now this man is telling me that he is going to the military in November. I felt myself getting hot and overcome with emotions. The air was on in the car but I still rolled down the window to get some fresh air.

"Brooke, babe, I'm doing this for us and for my son. I need to redirect my focus onto something different. I love rapping but let's be honest, everyone in Atlanta is a rapper. I'm tired of working at the collection agency and finding excuses as to why I cannot finish my AA. I'm trying to be the man you have asked me to become. You're going to be a doctor soon and I'm not trying to live off you. This was the only way I could do something and feel proud about doing it. You do understand that baby, right?"

As he was talking, I started to cry. I couldn't believe that God was finally answering my prayers about my relationship with Dee. I couldn't believe that this was same man I met three years ago at church, who was determined to be the next big rapper from Atlanta.

I wasn't upset anymore. Instead I was confused. I just knew that he wasn't the one for me. I just knew that he wasn't going to change his ways, but God proved me wrong. I sniffled as I reached over to hold his hand. At this point we had made it back to my apartment in Snellville and were still sitting in his car.

"I'm hurt that you didn't feel as if you could share this with me. I would've liked to have known this information before you shared it with my parents at dinner. You of all people should have known that I would've been happy for you. This is huge babe and I believe it is a step in the right direction," I managed to say through tears.

He leaned over and kissed my wet cheek. I turned in my seat to face him. Once we locked eyes, I leaned in to give him a kiss. He let out a soft moan as his hands begin to softly rub my thighs. He then moved his mouth down to my neck and it was my turn to let out a soft moan. His hands began to make their way to the middle of my legs. Luckily for him I had on a dress which made it easy for him to access my hidden treasure. He played down there for what seemed like forever. Every time I prepared to climax he would slightly move his hand back and allow me to catch my breath before starting back up again. This went on for about five minutes until he finally allowed me to get mine. I put my hand on the door handle and opened the door. Thank God his windows were tinted, I thought.

"I have to get up and teach Sunday school tomorrow. Were you planning on staying the night?" I asked breathlessly.

Instead of answering, Dee turned off his car and got out to head to my apartment. I lived on the first floor in the front, so we didn't have far to walk. I barely unlocked my front door before Dee had pushed me against it.

"What are you doing, sir? I told you I had to get ready for bed."

"And you will. But I wanted to help you get ready."

Those were his final words to me before he descended down to floor. With the ease of a smooth criminal, he removed my underwear and had my left leg propped up over his shoulder. His head got lost under my dress and in between my legs. His tongue moved slowly across my lady parts. I think he was spelling my full name down there!

I gripped the doorknob with one hand and used my other hand to further guide his head to my ecstasy. Somewhere mid-orgasm, I had been lifted off the ground and was firmly between him and my front door. I cried for mercy but he wouldn't relent. His tongue moved faster and faster, all while my body shook uncontrollably. He placed me down on the ground and took my hand to lead me to my sectional in the living room to continue what he had started.

The next morning, I left for church to teach my Sunday school class. Dee was still asleep when I left, but he would be attending the worship service later in the morning. I was glad to be alone for the twenty minute drive over to the church. I was able to release my tears freely as I chastised myself for having sex again.

Don't get me wrong, last night felt wonderful and I cannot remember making love so passionately to him. It was like our souls truly connected in a way that was divine. However, I knew there was nothing divine about what took place last night. I felt dirty and unworthy of God's grace. Not to mention I felt super nauseous before I left out of my apartment this morning.

Once I arrived at church, I sat in the car for a moment to gather myself. I had a few minutes to spare and decided to review the lesson for today. Ironically, the lesson was on abstinence and the reasons why we should wait to give our bodies.

"Really, God? You just couldn't have put a message in a bottle for me?" I thought.

There was no way I was going to present this message to my high school girls today; especially after what I did last night with Dee.

I looked at the message for the following week and it dealt with forgiveness. Again, I felt as if Jesus was slapping me all in my face. It took all that was in me not to say screw it and not teach my class this Sunday.

I was realizing I had a lot of issues and wasn't in the best position to teach these girls. How could I tell them to wait to have sex with their husbands, when I was getting it in with my boyfriend whenever I could? How could I teach them forgiveness when I didn't forgive Rashad for the hurt he caused me? I felt myself getting worked up again and then I found a lesson I could feel comfortable teaching.

Today's lesson would be on the purpose of tithing and offering. Something we all could learn a thing or two about.

Chapter 5

Rashad

"Objection! According to the rules of evidence, counsel is attempting to show negligence through subsequent measures," she stood up to say to the judge.

"*You gotta be freaking kidding me,*" I thought. I was standing before the judge, giving what had to be my best closing argument. By the look on the judge's face, she was confused by the objection as well.

"Denise, I would hope you never object to someone giving their closing argument. First of all, the rule allows for this type of evidence to come in to show ownership, control, or feasibility of precautionary measures. If you listen closely to his argument, you would've heard what exactly he was showing. Let's take a ten minute break and we'll get back to the closing arguments. We obviously need to practice those a little more."

I walked out of the classroom where we were having our mock trial practice to head to the bathroom. Before I could get out the door good, I felt a light tap on my shoulder. I turned to look down at one of the sexiest short women I knew with the prettiest green eyes looking up at me. Denise was as fine as they come. If we were in New Orleans she would be considered Creole because of her light skin. She usually kept her hair straightened but today she had this afro going on. She was one of the many girls who were going natural

However fine she was, I kept my distance from her. She was trouble. We tried dating during our first year of law school but things didn't work out as we planned. I had a hard time trying to stay focused on one woman. Denise came from big money and her family's political ties ran deep in the African-American community in Atlanta.

"That was terrible huh? Do you think Judge Stephens is mad at me?"

"Nah. You just got excited and thought you could trip your boy up."

She laughed and playfully rolled her at eyes at me.

"Whatever, Rashad. Anyways, what are you doing after practice?"

I could tell she wanted me to give her an invitation to hang out but I knew better than to do that with her. Obviously, my head below didn't get the memo that she was bad news.

"*Down boy*," I thought to myself. I was thankful to be wearing basketball shorts and was able to mask my growing erection. Before I could answer her, my cell phone buzzed. I reached in my pocket to grab it and saw that it was Natalie calling. What did she want? She knew I had practice today and that I was going to be unavailable for a few hours. I pressed ignore on my phone and continued talking with Denise.

"I'm probably going to go watch the game and-"

My phone buzzed. It was her again and I ignored her call again.

"Looks like someone is trying get a hold of you," Denise said, smiling.

I nodded my head but I didn't respond to her statement. Denise and I ended up talking until it was time for us to head back in the classroom to resume practice.

After practice was over, I checked my phone and saw three more missed calls from Natalie, along with a few text messages from her. The tone of her messages was accusatory and angry. I shook my head as I debated if I wanted to call her back.

These were the times that I questioned her sanity. It was like she had an extra dose of crazy in her and I was the crazy fool dating her. I didn't answer to her, but I did respect her enough to let her know when I was going to be out of pocket. It wasn't as if she didn't know I was going to be practicing. However, it was clear from her messages that she had a case of amnesia.

Once I made it to my car, I put my stuff in the trunk. As I closed the trunk and started walking to the front of my car, I heard hurried steps coming my way. I turned my head and was in utter shock to see Natalie approaching me.

"Why the hell did you not answer my calls or return any of my texts!" she spat at me once she got in my personal space.

I couldn't think of any words to say to her. I was stunned at the fact that she was here; which let me know she knew I had practice today. Why else would she be at the school on a Sunday? This was weird. Maybe this chick was crazy like my boy James told me.

I could tell she expected a response from me because she was still standing there with her arms crossed in front of her and her eyes attempting to pierce through my soul with her anger.

"Natalie," I spoke slowly, "You know I had mock trial practice. Where else would I be at? I told you that when I spoke to you last night. I even sent you a text this morning telling you I would be at practice. So I don't understand what your problem is, nor do I understand why you're here right now."

Now it was her turn to become silent. I could see the wheels in her head turning. It was as if she was trying to dissect what I was telling her. I could tell she was calming down as she moved her hands down to her sides. She ran her right hand through her black hair and put her head down for a moment.

"I forgot."

"How could you have forgotten? I told you several times. All you had to do was look at your text messages."

She lifted her head up to look me in my eyes. "I don't know, Rashad. I erase all of my text messages at night to free up space on my phone."

"But Nat, I texted you this morning. Are you going crazy, girl?"

"Don't call me crazy. You haven't seen crazy yet."

With that statement she turned and walked her crazy ass back to her car. I stood there still in complete and utter shock.

"Dude! You see that dunk! I promise KD put his balls all in my man's face!" James cackled as the sports station played an instant replay of the last play.

I took a swig of my beer. "Man, dude's face is going to smell like hot monkey balls for at least 30 more minutes! They still got too much time left in this half."

I was at the sports bar with James and some other guys from school watching the basketball playoffs. I was trying to forget the earlier part of my day with a night of drinking beer, watching sports, and trash talking. I was still processing the whole ordeal and was coming to the conclusion that Natalie might have some real issues. In the time I have known her, I've never seen her act the way she did. It was almost like she took a class in Stalker 101, the way she walked up on me in the parking deck.

I hadn't told James what happened because I had a feeling I knew what he was going to say. I figured it was best for me to leave what happened between Natalie and I in that parking garage. However, she was making that hard to do. She had been blowing up my phone with both calls and texts. I decided during halftime to return her call. I got up and went outside on the sport's bar patio.

"Hi, baby. I'm so glad you finally decided to call me back. I'm so sorry about earlier today," she said as soon as the call connected. I could tell that she had been crying by the tone in her voice.

I cleared my throat before responding to her.

"Natalie, what was that all about?"

"I don't know babe. I... I... I just wanted to see you. I knew you had practice, but I missed you. I came to the class where you were and I saw you talking to Denise. When I saw you talking to her I went back down to the computer lab to wait for you."

"Wait. You came by the classroom?"

This conversation was getting weirder by the minute. I wasn't even sure if she realized what she was saying to me. It was as if she was admitting to following me or something. As if she could sense what I was thinking, she began to clean up her statement.

"When I was calling you earlier I wanted to tell you that I was going to be up there. I had some research to do for my law review article. I was hoping to catch you and see if we could get together later this evening. I know that's not how it appeared by how I approached you, but it is the truth, babe."

It was hard for me to decipher if she was being truthful or not. My instincts told me that she was lying, but I had no proof to show me otherwise. I decided that it was best for me to leave it alone for now. I would file this situation in my memory bank and keep my eyes open from now on when dealing with her.

"It's cool, Nat. I'm about to go back in the bar and finish watching the game. I will try to call you when I leave here. If not, then we will talk tomorrow or something."

I heard her sniffle.

"That's fine, babe. Again I'm really sorry and I love you so much. Please forgive me."

"Yup. I holla at you later though."

I disconnected the call and walked back in the restaurant in time to catch the beginning of the third quarter. When I got back to my table, another round of beers had been ordered. I also noticed a couple females had migrated over to our table. As I got to closer to the table, I recognized Denise and another girl from our school with her.

"You done babysitting?" James whispered sarcastically.

I laughed and shook my head as I sat down in the chair next to him. Instead of responding to him, I chugged some of my beer. I didn't even have the energy to tell James about the phone call I had with Natalie. If I told him about the call, then I would have to tell him about what happened earlier. Again, I wasn't interested in reliving that moment. However, I was interested in figuring out what the odds were that Denise, the source of my trouble for the day, would be here tonight. As if she could hear my thoughts, she turned to me and smiled.

"Funny how things work out, huh?" she asked as she found a nearby empty chair and pulled it next to me.

I knew what she meant, but I decided to play coy. "What do you mean?"

She moved the chair she was sitting in closer to me. Her bare leg touching the outside of my long khaki shorts.

She cunningly smiled at me and said, "Well, my girlfriends and I always get together on Sundays to hang out. We usually take turns picking the place we're going to have drinks at. It's only four of us. Anyways, one of the girls is really into sports, so she picked this place."

I smirked. "Your friend part man or something? I don't know too many girls that voluntarily go to sports bar to watch games."

She playfully hit my arm as she laughed. "Shut up, Rashad!"

I couldn't help but laugh. "What I say wrong? You know I'm telling the truth. Ya'll just trying to get guys to buy ya'll drinks."

"Whatever boy! I will have you know that women are into sports just as much as guys. Plus, you already know I can take care of myself," she said with a wink.

I smirked at the latter part of her statement but I didn't say anything. I happened to look over at James, who was watching my interaction with Denise. He gave an approving look my way. Then I guess Denise turned her head for a moment, because James began to make a dry humping motion in his seat. One of the other boys saw it and started laughing. I put my head down to avoid busting out laughing.

"What's so funny?" Denise asked curiously, as she turned her attention back to the table. I looked over at her to see her putting something back in her purse, which was hanging on the back of her chair. She looked over at her girl who was doing a poor job of stifling her laugh. Nobody said anything and pretended to be engrossed in the game. I kept my attention on her and could tell she was becoming annoyed by not knowing what or who the joke was about.

"So what time are your other girls coming up here? It's getting kind of late," I said to her in order to shift her focus.

Denise shrugged her shoulders before looking down at her phone. She then turned her attention back to me. She still held that same look of annoyance in her eyes. I started to tell her what James had done, because I remembered how she used to get upset with me if she felt as if I was leaving her out of the loop.

Before I could say anything she said, "I text them just now. I forgot I had my phone in my purse. These two are always late. I swear they're going to show up late to their own funerals," she said shaking her head.

I chuckled at her frustration. We continued to watch the game and have small talk about nothing. Denise was a good girl when we dated a couple of years ago and was good people to be around. Although we didn't date long during our first year of law school, we still remained good friends. One thing I respected about her was that she didn't act entitled because she came from money. She never let the pedigree of her family dictate how she treated people. I remember Denise telling me that she was determined to make a name for herself and not live off the name of her family. That's where she and I could relate when it came to wanting to live outside the expectations set for you by others.

In my case, I was constantly trying to exceed my father's expectations. However, it was hard to do when I had no idea what he expected from me. At the end of the day, Denise was not the one.

"So can I tell you something?" she asked me with a slight hesitation in her voice. I nodded as she leaned over to whisper in my ear. "I want you, Rashad. Just for the night. No strings attached."

I remained stoned face with my attention still focused on the game highlights. I would be lying to myself if I said I didn't want her, but something told me that it was a bad idea to even entertain the thought of sleeping with her. Don't get me wrong, she was a great lay and all from what I remembered from when we were dating. However, one thing I didn't do was sleep with more than one woman at a time. I may get head from time to time, but I wasn't one for putting my Johnson all over the place.

After a few minutes, I turned to face Denise. I could tell she was confident that I was going to take her up on her offer.

"I'm not going to be able to do that," I said sincerely. "As much as I would love to take you home, I can't."

She sighed and shook her head. "I thought I would ask to see if maybe you were still the same."

I made an incredulous face and shook my head at her. I was almost insulted but then I thought about how a couple of weeks ago I had Natalie's roommate servicing me. Instead of responding to her, I got up, dapped up my boys, and left to go home for the night. By myself.

Chapter 6

Rashad

"Do you want dessert, babe?" I asked Natalie. She shook her head and continued to finish the rest of her steak. "We're good, man. You can just bring me the check when it's ready," I told our young waiter.

Natalie and I were having dinner at one of our favorite steakhouse restaurants in Downtown Atlanta. We had been spending time together since I got home on Sunday night from the sports bar. Ironically, she was in her car waiting outside of my apartment.

When I first saw her car I was pissed, but I thanked God that I didn't provide her with a copy of my house key. I also praised Him that I didn't take Denise up on her offer to bring her home with me. I jumped out of my car ready to go off on her but became speechless when I saw her get of her car. All she was wearing was a long, black trench coat with some black stilettos. Her hair was pulled up into a neat bun on top of her head and her lips were painted a deep red.

"What is the coat for? It's about 80 degrees out here," I remember asking her with a slick smile.

She never responded to my question. Instead she took my hand and led me upstairs to my apartment. Once inside she began to apologize in about 20 different ways. Now I would be lying to myself if I said I didn't enjoy being with her that night and for the past few nights after. However, I was still very concerned that she was off of her rocking chair and she had no intentions of getting back on it. Something told me that I needed to walk away from this relationship before things got crazy.

But here we sat having dinner together; three days away from the Greek picnic. The evening had been a pleasant one and I was enjoying her company. My mock trial team didn't have practice scheduled for this week because of a lot of conflicting priorities, so I had time to spend with Natalie.

I had been enjoying her company for these past few days. These times reminded me of how we were in the beginning of our relationship. I started to wonder why I couldn't give my complete all to her, but I was reminded of what happened in the parking deck.

"This was really nice, Shad. I'm so glad you suggested we come here for dinner tonight. We needed to get out of the house before a little bambino was made," Natalie said with a chuckle and took a sip of her wine.

I almost choked on my drink at her reference to a baby. This was the first time she had ever mentioned anything about a child. Marriage and children were topics of conversation I stayed away from with any female. I made it very clear to any woman I was dating that I wasn't looking to marry anytime soon, much less father any children.

I was extremely careful when it came to my escapades. The only exception I made was with Brooke. Brooke was different and I could see building a future with her.

At 17, I didn't really know anything about life. I was young, dumb, and full of cum. At least that's what I told myself whenever my mind began to wonder of what could have been with her.

Before I could respond to crazy Natalie, the waiter brought our check back to the table. *"Saved by the waiter,"* I thought as I got my wallet out.

"No, babe," Natalie said as she reached over to grab the bill away from me. "I will take care of it for you tonight. You always pay and treat me. Let me take care of this one for you tonight."

"You sure?" I asked with skepticism in my voice.

"Babe, it's the least I can do. Especially after how I started our week off. Let me do this for you."

Without any further discussion, I placed my credit card back in my wallet and enjoyed this rare moment. In the past year we had been dating, Natalie has never as much raised her hand to pay for anything. That was cool with me, because if there was one thing I knew how to do was take care of a woman. However, I was going to take advantage of her peace offering. I leaned over the table and gave her a quick kiss on the lips as my way of saying thank you.

The ride home from the restaurant was silent with the exception of the slow jams playing on the radio. I'm not sure what Natalie was thinking about, but I kept replaying the scene from Sunday in my head. It didn't make any sense to me. How did she forget I had practice? Has she ever popped up over my house and I not know about it? What was her perception when she saw me talking to Denise? These were a few of the questions brewing in my mind. I didn't ask any of them to her directly because I wanted to move on from the situation.

When I got to her apartment complex, I didn't bother to park. I didn't want her to think we were switching houses. I needed a moment away from her in order to think clearly about where I wanted this relationship to go.

"You aren't coming up for a little while?" she asked as she gathered her things off of the floor of my car.

"Nah. I'm going to head home and crash. I have a few things to do in the morning and I have to get ready for Parker and his girlfriend. They're supposed to be driving in tomorrow for the picnic."

She nodded her head and then turned to look at me. "I love you. You know that right?" she said with a catch in her voice. I could see her eyes starting to moisten.

"Of course. I love you too, Nat," I said with a gentle smile. I grabbed her hand and used it to help wipe a tear that had escaped from her eye.

"Okay. Well, I just want to make sure you know that. I would do anything for you and anything to keep you. You're a good man, Rashad."

"I try to be. Look, I'll call you when I get home to let you know I made it. Sometime tomorrow I will let you know what the plans are for this weekend."

She nodded again and leaned over to kiss me. Her kiss felt like one of desperation and I wasn't sure why she felt that way. I wasn't planning on leaving the relationship, at least not right now. I stayed in my car as I watched her walk to her door and go in her apartment. She gave me a wave, but I didn't leave until I saw her turn on her living room lamp.

Once I got back to my place, I took off my clothes and tossed them on the floor of my bedroom. I turned on the television and channel surfed for a while. Once I got bored of that I decided to play one of the new games I bought for my Xbox. I was in the middle of playing a multi-player game when my brother, Parker, called me.

"Yooo," I said as I watch my man die on the game.

"What up doe?" he responded.

"Hold on man. Let me switch over to my Bluetooth. I had my headset on for the game." I sat the phone down and reached over to my nightstand to get my Bluetooth off its charger. "Yeah. Hello?" I said as I fixed the volume on my Bluetooth.

"I'm here bruh. What are you over there playing?"

"Some zombie game man. I don't know. I picked it up last week. It's straight. I keep dying in the same spot though."

"That's cause you suck man," he cackled.

"Everyone ain't got time to sit around during their summer break and play games all day."

"And I do? Man, you just suck that's all and it's alright."

I sucked in a breath and rolled my eyes. I hurried and redirected the conversation before my brother turned into a whack version of Kevin Hart. He never really knew how to tell a good joke, but when he did tell one, he had a bad habit of not knowing when to end the joke.

"So, what's up Park?" I asked as I resumed playing my game.

"Nothing much man. I wanted to let you know that Bree and I will be in tomorrow night. I went ahead and took tomorrow off since we're driving down to Atlanta."

"Well, I bought an air mattress for you all to sleep- shit-on."

"You must have lost again." I did but I didn't say anything to him. My brother was bad luck. At least that's what I wanted to believe at that moment. "Well, we don't need the air mattress. We got a hotel room downtown."

I put my game controller down and turned my TV off. "For what?" I asked incredulously.

He cleared his throat. "Bree thought it would be wise to do so. Let's be honest man, she's going to want to see her sister. I'm pretty sure that Brooke isn't going to voluntarily come over to your place all willy nilly."

"That makes sense, I guess. I mean ya'll could have always went over there to see her. It's just pointless to spend money on a room if you don't have to." I was fuming with Brooke. If it's one thing I remembered from dating her, it's that she was bossy and liked things to go her way. I should've known she would have put a bug in her sister's ear. I could understand why she probably didn't want Bree staying at my place. Obviously, I was still her number one enemy. However, she didn't have the right to dictate where *my* brother stayed.

As if Parker could sense what I was thinking, he cleared his throat before he spoke again.

"It wasn't Brooke's idea. Bree spoke with her sister and she could tell it was upsetting for her. So in order to avoid any conflict, we decided it was best for us to stay in a hotel. That way it's a neutral setting for all involved."

"Again, I guess it makes sense. Is she afraid of running into me or something?"

"I mean let's be honest bruh. You got down to Georgia for school to play ball and slowly turned into a man whore. Almost like your old man. She saw through your b.s. and cut it off. I mean she was a little extreme with it, but you were wrong."

"It's been over five years. How long can a person carry a grudge?"

"I don't know man, but you better prepare yourself for this weekend. I think you two are going to have an encounter."

"Whatever man. I don't want to keep talking about her. What's up with Mom and Dad?"

"Nothing new. Mom has been in court this week. Your father, on the other hand, has had this influx of speaking engagements. The summer is usually his down time, so I'm not sure he's going to do the work of the Lord."

I shook my head. "Pops is cold blooded. I can't wait for the day for him to be exposed. Does Mom even question him anymore?"

"Well, here's the funny thing. Mom has been real low key. When I go over there to visit them, she puts on this happy face. I mean I have tried to hint around to her that I think Pops is doing wrong, but she always changes the subject."

"Hmm. So who has been doing the preaching?"

"I do the Bible studies for the time he's gone during the week. Then on Sundays Pastor Johnson and I have been alternating. I mean, his screwing around is helpful for me, because I get to share God's word. So I'm not necessarily complaining."

Parker has wanted to preach ever since I can remember. He's currently finishing up seminary school in Dallas. When we were kids, he would want to play church. One day he was acting like he got the Holy Ghost and fooled around speaking in tongues for real! I was so scared, because I didn't know what was going on. I thought for sure the rapture or something was getting ready to take place.

We talked a little while longer in order to finalize the plans for the weekend. When I got off the phone with him, I started thinking about the probability of seeing Brooke this weekend. A big part of me hoped to see her. I didn't know what I would say or do if I did see her. I knew one thing for sure. If I saw her again, I wasn't letting her walk out of my life again.

Chapter 7

Brooke

I never quite understood why it always felt as if people assumed I wanted them to unburden themselves at my expense. I've always been that friend who held everyone's deepest and darkest secret. At times I felt as if I was going to explode with all the information I was holding and spew toxic waste on anyone who crossed my path.

Today I was feeling as if I was going to unload my own. I was agitated because my period was still playing hide and seek with me and I was still at work. I was at the community center where I mentored a few high school girls. I usually talk to them about taking care of their bodies, provide encouragement regarding their scholastic goals, and help them get comfortable with changes as they matured into young women. Today, however, I had planned to meet with the girls, make my case notes, and get home to prepare for the weekend.

The Greek picnic was tomorrow and my sister was coming to see me before heading to her hotel for the night. It had been a while since I had gotten out of the house and did something completely unrelated to medical school. However, one of my girls stopped me after our group session and wanted to talk privately.

"Ms. Brooke, I don't know who else to talk to and I really need some advice," Michelle said once we got to the office I used.

Michelle Diaz was a beautiful young lady of Puerto Rican and African-American descent. She was often quiet during our group sessions but when she did participate in the discussions I found her to be very intelligent; which was not surprising as she attended one of Atlanta's most prestigious high schools. However, the look on her face led me to believe that her issue was not school related.

"What's going on, Michelle? Is everything okay?"

She sighed deeply and shook her head. I motioned for her to sit on the couch as I took a seat in the recliner across from her. For a moment we sat there in silence. I could tell that she was still trying to decide if I was the right person to open up to about whatever was going on. I was patient with my girls. I never rushed them to tell their story or issues in our group discussions, but today I was ready to go and I needed her to get to talking.

I hated to rush her but if she wasn't going to talk, then I was going to go home and get some rest before my weekend got started.

"Michelle, if you want to come back another time that's okay," I sweetly said.

"I'm pregnant, Ms. Brooke."

I wasn't sure I heard her correctly. "Excuse me?"

"I'm pregnant. I'm almost in my second trimester. I haven't told anyone and I've been able to hide it so far. But I don't think that I'm going to be able to hide it much longer. I don't graduate until next year and the baby is due in January. I just don't know what I'm going to do."

At this point she was crying and wouldn't look up at me. I was at a loss of words. Why was everybody pregnant around me? For some reason I couldn't picture her having sex let alone having unprotected sex. She was too smart for this type of mistake. I knew her parents were going to rock her world once they found out she was pregnant.

"Michelle... How...well I know how it happened," I said gently. "But what happened?"

"I was with my boyfriend. He was a virgin. It was our first time. The condom broke but we kept on going." She sighed and continued speaking. "We were just so caught up in the moment. It was only one time, Ms. Brooke. It was my first time having sex ever and I'm pregnant."

"Wow," was all I could manage to say at the moment.

I closed my eyes and began to rub my temples. I hoped that I could find the right words to say to her, but I had nothing. All I knew was that her life was getting ready to take a turn and I could only pray that it would be a positive outcome for her. She sniffled loudly and I heard her fumble around in her purse. I opened my eyes in time to see her take a bottle of pills out of her purse.

"What are those?" I asked.

"These are the prenatal vitamins I got from the health clinic. Jerome and I got to see the baby yesterday."

"Michelle, what do you think you should do?"

"I heard the baby's heart beating, Ms. Brooke." she smiled, sweetly. "I was originally going to get an abortion. I didn't want to hinder myself. When I heard my baby's heartbeat, I knew that I couldn't go through with the abortion. Jerome told me not to kill our baby and that he would do whatever he has to do to take care of us."

I sighed heavily. "Well, you need to tell your parents. Both of you need to let your parents know that you're pregnant. I'm not going to lie to you Michelle, its going to be very hard. You're so young and have so much life ahead of you still. I don't advocate abortions, but I do hope you're sure of the decision you're making. I'm going to be here for you. If you want to tell your parents here at the center because you feel as if you would be in a safe environment, you can do that."

"I'm going to tell them this weekend. I think my mother knows. She keeps making weird comments about how if I ever got pregnant she would be disappointed, but she would help me. I'm more concerned about Jerome."

"Why is that?"

"Well, he has a full basketball scholarship and he's leaving for school this coming fall. I'm not sure how this is going to affect him."

I pursed my lips together. I knew that Jerome would be fine, because he wasn't the one carrying the baby. He could still pursue his dreams and it would be very easy for him to leave Michelle hanging. I haven't met him but he seemed like he cared about Michelle and their unborn child based upon this conversation with her. However, I know how great temptations can be and how easy it is for men to check out of a relationship. It happened to me with Rashad and I didn't even have a baby. Dating an athlete is hard and God forbid he's a starter. You can forget it! I prayed for her sake that Jerome came from a good family who had an ounce of morality.

"Michelle," I cleared my throat. "I want you to figure out what you're going to do regarding your education. Let that be your focus. That is what your parents are going to be more concerned with because you still have to graduate next year from high school."

She nodded her head in agreement and sighed heavily as I assumed she was processing what I said. We talked for a little while longer about her situation and came up with a game plan. We decided that we would get both sets of grandparents together at the center to tell them. She had texted Jerome to inform him of what we had planned and he agreed to get his parents down to the center next week after they had returned from their family vacation in Jamaica. In the meantime, Michelle was going to work with her guidance counselor to get information on what she could do regarding her school work during the time she would be out after having the baby.

Later that evening, I was getting a foot massage from Donovan at his place. I wanted to spend some time with him before my sister arrived tomorrow. I also wanted to talk with him about how I had been feeling after we had sex. My conversation with Michelle had me shook big time. It reminded me of what my parents used to say to me about waiting to have sex before marriage.

Although I'm grown and could pop out as many babies as I wanted, I knew that it was not wise for me to do so. I had goals and aspirations to achieve. A child would slow me down. At the time I wasn't even sure if I wanted to have any children. Plus I knew having sex with Donovan was going against the principles that had been instilled in me from church. I was tired of feeling guilty about having sex with someone I knew was not going to be my husband.

"Dee, can we talk for a minute?" I asked with a slight hesitation in my voice. He immediately stopped rubbing my feet but held them gently. I could see in his eyes there was apprehension, but he smiled as he nodded at me. I sighed deeply. "I want us to stop having sex."

He erupted in laughter. I mean this fool threw his head back and laughed from his soul. I wasn't sure what was so funny and wait…is that a tear coming from his eye?!

"Bae, you can't be scaring me like that. I thought it was about some life or death type of sh-… stuff. Girl, you are funny. Why would you want to do that, Brooke?"

I rolled my eyes and stood up so I could create some distance between us. I was two seconds from smacking his black tail for laughing at me.

"First of all, I don't know why you're laughing at me. I'm so serious, Donovan. I want us to stop having sex. I'm not interested in sleeping with you unless we're married. It's messing with me." I narrowed my eyes at him and continued my point. "Do you know after each time, I'm somewhere crying my eyes out? I feel horrible after we have sex. How can I expect God to bless me and I can't stop myself from going there with you?"

He wasn't laughing anymore. I could see that he was stunned by what I had dropped on him. He clearly didn't know I felt like crap after each time we slept together. I never told him and I hadn't planned on telling him. But after talking with Michelle and crying on my way to the church earlier that week, I couldn't continue carrying on the way I had.

"Why are you crying? Do you not like it or something?"

I rolled my eyes. Did this man miss what I said to him? I sighed and shook my head.

"It has nothing to do with you and your performance in bed. I'm feeling convicted and I don't want to have sex anymore without a change in my last name. I'm not asking you to marry me or anything, but-"

"What if I wanted to ask you?" he interrupted me.

I made a confused face. "Ask me what?"

"To marry me?"

Now it was my turn to laugh.

"Stop playing, Dee. I'm being serious and you're up here making jokes," I said laughing.

"I'm not playing. I'm serious, Brooke, marry me. We could get married tomorrow if that's what you wanted. I love you and I know for sure that you're the woman I want to spend the rest of my life with. Marry me, Brooke."

Then he stood up and got down on one knee. I'm not sure where the tears came from but I knew they weren't necessarily tears of joy. I was confused. This wasn't how I expected this conversation to go. I hoped that he would be angry or do something stupid, so I could take an easy out. This wasn't part of the plan at all.

"You don't have a ring," was all I could manage to say.

He snapped his fingers and got up to head to his room. I heard him open up one of his dresser drawers. When he made it back into the living room, I had sat back down on the couch. I was trying to figure a way out of this proposal. The last thing I wanted to do was marry him. Don't get me wrong, I love him with all my heart, but I still was on the fence about him being the one.

Dee came and got back down on one knee. This time he presented me with a small velvet box. I watched him open it and I saw the most beautiful ring. I'm not sure where he got the money from but it wasn't a cheap ring. I stared at the platinum, princess cut diamond, surrounded by begets going around the band.

"So, let me ask you again," he said, taking my left hand. "Will you do me the honor of becoming of my wife? I don't want you to feel that way ever again. I love you, Brooke."

I closed my eyes and nodded. Maybe he was the one and God was answering my prayers in regards to our relationship. At least that's what it seemed like and I was going to roll with it until the wheels the fell off.

Chapter 8

Rashad

The infamous Greek Picnic weekend had arrived and the festivities were in full effect. I had only missed one or two Greek picnics since I crossed into my frat and had been living in Georgia. It was always great networking and meeting others frat brothers but let's be honest, it was all about the women.

There were so many beautiful black women that came to Atlanta for this weekend and a brother had his pick of any flavor he wanted. Chocolate, mocha, and sometimes there were hints of vanilla sprinkled in the mix, but you definitely had to be careful when making your selection. HIV and other STDs were real. There were a few times I had been reckless. I always thanked my lucky stars that I hadn't caught anything or knocked someone's daughter up. I made sure to get tested every six months.

This year was different for me. I wouldn't be on the patrol for new booty. I was in an actual relationship and my girl was going to be lurking around. Even if I wanted to hook up with anyone else, I knew that the chances of getting caught were great. Plus she almost messed up my day with her early morning drama.

"So, I'm not understanding why we can't go to the picnic together," she pouted in my room earlier that day.

I sighed heavily and closed my eyes. I hoped that when I opened my eyes she would be gone, but lo and behold, she was still lying next to me in the bed. I knew I shouldn't have let her stay the night, I thought to myself.

"Helllllo! Rashad, I'm asking you a question. What is the problem? I'm here and we might as well use one car."

Again, I sighed heavily and sat up in the bed.

"Nat, I'm not doing this with you. I have to start getting ready and you know that I'm hanging with my boys. I told you that we would get together tomorrow. You were cool with this last night before we went to sleep. So what the hell is the problem now?"

"You need to watch who you're talking to. I'm not some side chick that yo…"

"What the hell are you talking about now?" I said, cutting her off. "Who said anything about a side chick? You're tripping, man." I got out the bed and started towards the bathroom. Natalie was right on my heels, still fussing.

"But that's what you're implying right now. You think that you can screw me and discard me like a piece of trash. Well, I'm here to let you know that you got the wrong one!"

This girl was crazy. I'm not sure where she got this side chick business from, especially when all I did was reiterate what we talked about less than 24 hours ago.

"I just want to take a piss in peace, Natalie. If that's alright with you?" I asked as I lightly placed my hand on her right shoulder to move her out of the way to close the

bathroom door. Before I could even get my hand on her shoulder good she smacked my hand down. Hard.

"Don't put your hands on me! Are you crazy?" she hollered.

I stepped back and I looked at her in shock, trying to figure out who she was. I shook my head and went to the toilet to handle my business. She stood in the doorway looking like she wanted to rip my dick from my body. I flushed the toilet and walked over to the sink to wash my hands. I couldn't believe this girl was tripping out the way she was. It was as if she was possessed by some type of demon.

I attempted to walk around her to get out of the bathroom, but she blocked me. It took everything in me to keep my hands by my side and not shake the mess out of her.

Through gritted teeth, I asked, "Can you please move?"

Instead of moving out of my way, she hugged me. Again, I was rendered speechless. Less than five minutes ago she was ready to square up with me now she was hugging me as if all was well. This girl might really be as crazy as my boy James said.

"I'm sorry. I shouldn't have acted that way. You hate me now?"

I sighed and shook my head. Just crazy as hell, I thought to myself. I still didn't know what to say, but I was smart enough not to awaken Dr. Jekyll.

"No," was all I said. Then suddenly my chest felt warm and wet. Damn. Why is she is crying now? "What's wrong, Natalie? Why are you crying?"

"I know I keep messing up. I'm trying so hard, Shad. I just want to be with you all the time and I realize that's not realistic."

"Have I ever given you a reason not to trust me?"

"No, but I've seen things and sometimes I just don't know if I should trust you."

"She's seen things? What the hell does that mean?" I thought to myself. Clearly she must have meant to say she heard things and not seen things. Not that either one was better than the other, but seeing things meant I was slipping or she was stalking me. The latter didn't sit well with me.

I stepped back in the bathroom and folded my arms across my chest. I narrowed my eyes and asked, "What do you mean you've seen things?"

A puzzled look came across her face. For a moment I swore the color in her skin went pale. She quickly recovered. "I meant to say I heard things, babe."

I didn't have any proof, but the thought that Natalie may be stalking me was starting to become more plausible.

We stood in silence for what felt like an eternity. Natalie's focus was on her freshly pedicured feet which were getting wet from the tears flowing from her eyes. I knew her mind was working in overdrive but she almost blew me away with her next question.

Natalie looked up at me with red eyes. She sniffled and asked, "So you've never been with Tori?"

I made an incredulous face. "Your roommate, babe? Where did you hear that? No, baby. How and why would I do something like that? Does that even make sense to you?"

Natalie closed her eyes and breathed deeply. "Okay babe."

I closed the distance between us and kissed the top of her head. She was watching me. I didn't have any hardcore proof, but I wasn't as up on my game as I thought I was. The last thing I needed was to get caught up in some fatal attraction type drama.

I arrived at the Greek Picnic with Parker and James later that afternoon. I was able to get rid of Natalie fairly easily after I assured her that we would spend all day Sunday together. Although, I would rather watch paint dry than spend time with her. I was really beginning to think that she was certifiably crazy. It was very possible that she had a certificate of crazy waiting for her in the mailbox. I wasn't interested in finding out one way or the other. I figured it was best for me to lay low for a while and keep a mental tab on her behavior for a little while.

Once we parked at the picnic, my mind was no longer on Natalie and all her antics. There were too many beautiful women to look at. I even ran into Denise while I was party hopping with some frat. She looked good in her green shorts and pink polo top, dancing with a few of her sorority sisters. When she saw me and waved, I waved back but kept it moving. I knew that Natalie was going to be at the picnic at some point, if she wasn't already. The last thing I needed to deal with was her accusing me of sleeping with Denise. She already thought I was smashing her roommate. I'm still trying to figure out how she would get that type of information.

The guys and I ended up hanging out where our frat and sorors were set up. One of the frat brothers had the grill going and there were some picnic tables set up. As I observed everything around me, I felt old. Most of the folks there were still in college getting there first degree and had freshly pledged. I was only 26 but I could tell that I was light years ahead of a lot of them. I knew that most of them were there to hook up with other people. No one was really looking to settle down. But for some reason I was beginning to think about it, slowing down. I saw a lot of my father's ways in myself and I knew if I didn't slow down I was going to turn into the man I despised so much.

My self-reflecting was interrupted by Parker letting me know they were getting ready to bless the food. After Parker said the prayer, we all got in line to fix our plates. The frat and sorors went all out with the food selection. There were ribs, chicken, hot dogs, potato salad, baked beans, and all types of desert. It was times like this I was grateful for my high metabolism. We made our plates and lucked up on a table that was under the shade.

"Man, I was so hungry!" James said. "I was beginning to wonder if I was going to have to steal one of the finished trays of chicken wings."

We all started laughing. Parker, with his mouth full of baked beans said, "These crazy black people would have beat your butt if you did that. I know you know not to play with black people and they food."

"Yeah man," I said laughing, "You're outnumbered here. It ain't nothing but a hand full of ya'll here. Don't be trying nothing stupid like that."

"Speaking of stupid, man," James said. "I see your girl walking our way."

"Quit playing dawg," I said with a mouthful of chicken.

Both Parker and I turned around to see if James was joking. Sure enough, it was Natalie, her cousin Rochelle, Bree, and some other girl walking towards our table.

"Oh shoot man." Parker said. "Brooke is coming over. You gonna be alright man?"

"Thee Brooke?" James asked in disbelief. "The one who got away?"

"Yup," Parker responded smugly.

As the ladies approached our table, my whole body tensed up as I tried to get a good look at Brooke without Natalie noticing. She looked beautiful. She was wearing a white fitted shirt that had her sorority letters written in blue. Ironically, she was my soror. She kept her arms folded across her chest. I could tell she was uncomfortable and trying her best to act as if I wasn't sitting in front of her. I couldn't tell what she was looking at because her sunglasses were dark.

Brooke's hair had grown so much and she now had blonde highlights. That was not the only thing that had grown either. I could tell she had put on more weight from college. She wasn't fat but she was definitely thick in all the right places. Then my eyes caught a sparkle coming from her left hand. I felt my heart sink. She's married?

"Hi, baby," Natalie said in a sing song voice.

She draped her long arms around my neck and planted a wet kiss on my lips. She positioned her body in front of mine and kept smiling. I could tell she wanted to me tongue her done in front of everybody. As usual, she was being extra.

Before I could muster any words to speak, Brooke whispered something in Bree's ear and walked off towards the restrooms. I had to make my move. Discretely, of course. I turned to Natalie and asked if she wanted me to fix her plate or get her a drink. She told me she was fine and was going to sit at the table with her cousin. They were just stopping by to say hey to us and had planned to stop at her sorority's section next.

"Well, I'm going to head to the bathroom real quick and grab me another drink on the way back," I informed her with a kiss to her lips.

The bathrooms were located on the other side of the park; which was a great thing. I had to thank the universe for such a perfect set up. I could still run the risk of getting caught, but it was a chance I was willing to take.

By the time I made over to the bathroom, I actually had to use it. The bathrooms were side by side with a water fountain in the middle. As fate would have it we came out of the bathroom at the same time. This time Brooke's glasses were pushed on top of her head and her eyes were red.

"Hi, Brooke," I said softly.

"Rashad," she said dryly.

Brooke pulled her glasses down over her eyes. For a moment I thought she was going to walk off but she stood there. We were silent for a moment. I was looking at the ground and kicking an imaginary rock, trying to find words to say to her. I looked up when she cleared her throat.

"So, you're Natalie's Shad?"

Her statement was more rhetorical than it was a question to me. I nodded my head. I wanted to tell her that I was always her Shad and that I never stopped loving her, but her phone rang and she answered the call. I took that as a sign and headed back to where our folks were. When I made it back to the picnic area, I made sure to grab a soda from the ice chest. It appeared that Natalie had stayed put and that my little absence was not missed. I briefly caught my brother's eye and he nodded at me. I shook my head.

Brooke eventually came back to the table and sat down with a plate of food. Her glasses were pulled back up, but this time there wasn't any trace of tears. There was also a visible shift in her demeanor. She seemed to have calmed herself and was more relaxed.

"Oh snap!" Brooke exclaimed. "Come on, Bree! That's our song. They're already strolling."

Brooke got up and grabbed Bree's hand. They took off to where the other frat and sorors who were forming a joint stroll line. I seized the moment to head over there and get in line with them. I got right behind Brooke with Bree behind me. I guess Parker and James followed me over, because I noticed that Parker was behind Bree. James was rhythmically challenged and stood with some other frat brothers looking on.

When the stroll was over Brooke turned and hugged me. She was sweating and laughing. Damn she is fine, I thought as we stood face to face again. She had a playful look in her eyes. I think for a second that she forgot that I was her number one enemy and was caught up in the moment.

"Just like old times, huh?" she winked and smiled at me before walking off with her sister.

I wasn't sure what old times she was referring to but I was like a kid in a candy store. I must have forgot that Natalie was watching me and I would soon be reminded that I needed to always be on my guard.

Chapter 9

Brooke

Before the Greek picnic

"I can't believe you said yes," my sister said, shaking her head in disbelief at me.

We were at my apartment lounging around in my living room before getting ready to head to the Greek picnic. Parker had dropped her off early in the morning before heading to hang with his brother. I was filling her in on what had transpired in the last 48 hours. I was a nervous wreck because there was no way I was going to be able to avoid Rashad today.

"Well, at least he got you a nice ring," she said, grabbing my hand to inspect my ring for the millionth time.

"Bree," I sighed, pulling my hand back. "My issue isn't that I accepted Dee's proposal. My issue right now is Rashad."

My sister waved her hand and rolled her eyes at me as she sat back on the couch.

"I don't know why, Brooke," she said, matter-of-fact. "You knew this day was going to come at some point. Atlanta is big, but it ain't that big. And since we are talking about him, I feel like you need to know that he goes to Emory's law school."

My eyes got big and my mouth dropped wide opened. I started to ask her why didn't she tell me this before, but I quickly remembered that I cut her off every time she tried to tell me anything related to him.

I moaned in defeat at my nightmare becoming my reality in a few hours.

"What am I going to do Bree?" I whined to my sister.

"You're so dramatic lately, Brooke! You'll be fine. I got your back and I'm going to be right there with you. We can't avoid the Sigma section all day. We have to go over there at some point to greet the sorors and other frat. Who knows? It may be so many folks there that we won't run into the guys at all."

I pouted as I sighed deeply. This day was going to be interesting. It had already started out interesting before my sister had arrived to my place. My cycle still was missing in action and at this point, I knew that it was time for me to come out of my denial. I was mulling over in my head how I was going to break the news to her. I still hadn't told Donovan that I was carrying his child. There was no question about whether I was going to keep the baby or not.

"I'm pregnant," I said softly. I kept my eyes focused on my hand so not to look at her. I heard Bree make a choking sound as she sat her drink back on the table. In my peripheral I could see her trying to regain her breathing by placing her hand her chest. Now she was the one being dramatic.

"What did you say? Did you say you're pregnant?" she asked as she managed to pull herself together.

I nodded my head before turning to look at her. Her dark brown eyes looked like they were going to pop out of her head at any moment. Her mouth would open and then close. I could tell she had several questions for me but had to think of where to begin.

"Yes, It's Dee's baby. I'm probably about six or so weeks now. I go for my first ultrasound on Tuesday. Pat is going to do it. I haven't told anyone but you, and yes, I'm going to keep the baby."

This time she nodded at me. We sat in silence for a few moments. I wasn't sure what my sister was thinking, but I was happy to have this burden lifted off of my shoulders. I knew I was pregnant the night I came back from the club with Natalie and Rochelle a few weeks ago. It was this morning before my sister arrived that I finally decided to take a test. It was positive before the strip had a chance to dry completely. I cried so hard.

"Brooke," Bree said sweetly as she took my hand.

She gave me a gentle squeeze and I squeezed her hand back as we sat there quietly. The only sounds being made were our sniffles, as tears rolled down both of our faces. I didn't know what my sister's tears were for, but I knew exactly what mine were for.

I wasn't sure how I was going to finish medical school. I still had a year left and then another four years to complete my residency program. I was so disappointed in myself. If only I had been stronger and kept my legs closed. If only I would have walked away from Dee when I found out about Sheba and Justice. I wouldn't be in this situation now. All the should of's, could of's and would of's weren't enough to erase my reality.

All of sudden, Bree stood up and pulled me up with her.

"Come on, sis. We have to get dressed. Otherwise we are going to be in this house all day crying," she said with a warm smile. I smiled back and nodded my head.

"My feet are hurting me," Natalie complained as we were walking into the picnic.

"*If your dumb behind hadn't worn stilettos to a stupid picnic they wouldn't hurt,*" I thought.

We had just arrived to the Greek Picnic two hours after it got started because Natalie was late getting to Rochelle's apartment. We waited at least another hour for her to arrive and she still had the nerve to not be ready when she got there. She wanted to wear something out of Rochelle's closet which meant she had to change her makeup to coordinate with the new outfit.

Now she was wearing a pair of mini shorts and a red and white halter top. To top off her outfit she was wearing a pair of red stilettos. Natalie's shorts were so short they could have been mistaken for underwear. I know her founders had to be rolling over in their graves. Thankfully, she didn't wear any letters to the picnic.

The rest of us were dressed more casual for the picnic. We all wore a fitted t-shirt with our respective sorority logo and a pair shorts. I had to find something that could fit because all of sudden my clothes were not fitting properly. Luckily, I was able to still fit my favorite sorority shirt and a pair of blue jean shorts.

Bree was making it a point to stay very close to my side and being overly protective of me. At one point I thought I was going to have to slap her when she snatched a Coke out of my hand.

"What the hell, Bree?" I said as I tried to reach for my drink back.

"You know you can't be drinking this crap," she said through gritted teeth.

Thankfully the other girls were preoccupied and not paying attention to our sisterly spat. I rolled my eyes as I reached in the cooler for a bottle of water. I shook the water bottle in Bree's face as I walked past her to stand next to Rochelle. She appeared to be fascinated at her cousin attempting to stroll with her sorors in her stilettos.

"I cannot believe she wore that outfit," she said with a chuckle.

I shook my head and let out a soft laugh as I remembered when we first crossed over into our sorority. You couldn't tell me we weren't hot stuff. My line sisters used to get on the big sisters' nerves with our antics.

I remember one time our whole line had been kidnapped by the big brothers. It just so happened that Rochelle was dating one of them. He got the bright idea to hold her as ransom. Talk about pissed! I'm still not sure how they captured our whole line, but we worked together to break free.

"Well, remember we were young once. We used to have to compete with the other girls on campus," I said laughing.

"Hmph. Well, I don't like it. You can tell who her line sisters are because they're all dressed semi slutty," Rochelle said with disdain in her voice.

"If I recall correctly, someone was a tad bit slutty in our hay day. I distinctly remember getting kidnapped to save someone."

"Oh, no you didn't go there, Brooke!" Rochelle said, playfully hitting my arm.

Finally, Natalie was done strolling with her sorority sisters and walked over to where we were standing. I noticed she had taken off her shoes and was walking around the park barefoot. To be so smart and cute, she was really about as dumb as a bag of rocks.

"Man, I still got it y'all," Natalie said to no one in particular.

I rolled my eyes and shifted my weight. I was getting more annoyed by the second. The heat wasn't helping my pregnant self at all and I really needed to find somewhere to sit. Before I could suggest that we find a place to relocate, Natalie made a discovery that I wished she would've kept to herself.

"Oh look! I see the guys! I didn't that think we would run into them. Let's go over there and see what they're up to. I know you guys want to hang with your folks."

Bree quickly turned to me and flashed a warm smile my way. I knew it was her way of telling that she had my back. I smiled back at her and hooked my arm through hers.

My heart almost stopped beating when I saw him. I wasn't ready, but there he was standing before me. Rashad was wearing long, blue jean shorts with a blue and white polo. His outfit complimented his smooth dark skin. I also noticed that he had grown his hair out into neat locs. Had he finally grown a goatee? I remember he used to pencil in his facial hair to make it connect when we were in high school.

Rashad was a sight to behold. Natalie practically threw herself all over him. It was just like her to be so damn extra. I could tell he was uncomfortable and made a feeble attempt to distance himself from her.

"Hi baby," I heard Natalie say to him.

He was still standing there looking stupid. All of sudden, I felt nauseous. I had to get to the bathroom quickly before I threw up in front of everyone. I whispered to Bree that I had to go to the restroom.

"Do you need me to go with you?" she asked with a genuine concern.

"I can throw up by myself, but thank you for being willing to join me, sister of mine," I said with a smile.

Bree playfully rolled her eyes and went back to the group. I almost broke out into a sprint to make to the bathroom. I barely made it to the toilet before everything started coming up. Although I figured it was my hormones causing me to throw up, I knew that my nerves were really the culprit. Seeing Rashad made me nervous. I could feel my heart racing as beads of sweat fell from my forehead. I flushed the toilet and walked over to the sink and I washed my hands before rinsing out my mouth. I reached in my purse for a piece of gum. I also found a Zofran that I swallowed without any water.

As I walked out the bathroom, I ran into Rashad. Thankfully the Zofran had started to work immediately, but that didn't stop my heart from racing and the sweat from forming. We didn't say anything to each other for a few moments. It felt like an eternity standing there looking at him.

"...Hi, Brooke," he said softly.

"Rashad." was all I could manage.

He looked down at the ground and began to kick his feet. I knew he was nervous and my tone wasn't inviting. Then something dawned on me. I cleared my throat.

"So, you're Natalie's Shad."

Before he could respond, my phone rang in my purse. I knew from the ring tone that it was Donovan. I answered the phone without any hesitation. Rashad slightly nodded and headed back to the picnic area.

"What's up, babe?" I asked as I answered the phone. I didn't try to hide my annoyance with his calling me.

"I'm sorry sweets to be calling you. I know you're out with your girls. I'm trying to find clippers at your apartment and I can't seem to find them."

"Oh, I think I moved them out of the bathroom and forgot to put them back. Look under the sink."

"...Got them. Alright. Love you, babe."

"Love you, too."

For some reason, after my call with Donovan I felt re-energized as I headed back to the picnic area. Once I arrived to where my sister and friends were, the DJ had put on a joint stroll song. Some of the frat and sorors were already forming the stroll line. I had to get in on the action. Part me wanted to show Rashad what he was missing out on.

"Oh snap!" I exclaimed to Bree. "Come on!" I said as I grabbed her hand and pulled her over to the stroll line.

Rashad and Parker joined us and Rashad got right behind me. I looked over to my left where Natalie was standing and she was watching him tough. I turned my head back to the front of the line and smirked. There was a part of the stroll dance where the girls backed it up and dropped it on the guys. I made sure to give a little extra for my one man audience. I don't know why I was acting like I was in secret competition with Natalie for Rashad. I mean, I had a fiancé and I was going to be a mother, but for a moment I forgot about everything and everyone. I was reliving the love I felt for Rashad. This was Dallas. We were kids having fun.

Once the song ended, I turned and hugged Rashad. I was sweating, but I was giddy.

"Just like old times. Huh?" I said with a wink and a smile.

He simply smiled at me. I laughed and walked off with my sister.

Part 2
The Storm

Chapter 10

Rashad

Fall 2010

I had four months left until graduation. However, I decided that I was going to take the bar next summer. My plan was to continue working with the law firm that I interned with since after my first year. A part of me wanted to take the entire spring and sleep my life a way, but I knew that sleeping wasn't going to pay my bills.

Things between Natalie and I were going well. Her insecurities seemed to have calmed down about me cheating on her. I cut my ties with Tori. I had to admit that was too close to home and it would've only been a matter of time before I got caught up. Plus we had a huge blow up after the Greek picnic concerning me strolling with Brooke.

"That trick had her ass all over of you like she wanted to do you right there on the grass!" she screamed at me.

We were at my apartment and were both yelling at the top of our lungs. I couldn't believe I was going back and forth with her, but I knew that I couldn't tell her that Brooke was my ex. That was a secret I had to take to the grave. At the rate we were going, I felt like she was trying to send me to an early one.

"Natalie, I'm not doing this bullshit with you! You've seen me do that stroll a thousand times. Why all of the sudden is it an issue? Get out here with that," I said in a dismissive tone.

"You're right but for some reason this time it looked like you knew her. Then that hoe turned around and hugged you like you two were BFFs!"

I sighed heavily and closed my eyes. I knew I was tired of fighting this losing battle with Natalie. I had to think of a way to calm her down and then get her out of my apartment.

"Look. I don't know her. I know that she's Bree's sister. Bree happens to date my brother. I didn't notice her dancing any different than any other girl that was there. I wouldn't do anything to disrespect you."

I grabbed her hand and pulled her into me. I leaned down and gave her kiss on the lips. I could feel her body become relaxed as I kissed her. She broke our kiss and looked up at me with harsh eyes.

"I don't believe you, but I can't prove you did anything wrong, so I'm going to give you the benefit of the doubt. I swear Rashad, if you're lying to me…"

While shaking her head at me, she pushed me back. I was a least 140 pounds heavier than her so I didn't move at all.

"You swear what Natalie?" I said as I kissed her neck. "That you'll punish me or something?"

All she could do was moan and nod her head. I could tell she wanted to say something, but I kept distracting her. I kept my eyes closed and imagined that I was kissing Brooke and it was Brooke I was getting ready to make love to.

"You know Georgia is coming for Bama this year!" I said as I sat down on my couch and turned on the television.

"Shad, we are not about to have this discussion. Georgia cannot beat Alabama, unless they recruit Jesus to play every available position," James said calmly as he took a swig of his beer.

James and I were hanging out at my place. We had mock trial practice earlier that morning and made sure that we finished early enough to watch the big game. A couple of other fellas from our school were supposed to come by to chill as well. This was a going to be a welcomed break for me.

I was starting to feel overwhelmed with these last few classes, preparing for the mock trial competition, and working almost full-time at the law firm. Outside of practice, this was the first weekend I had to relax. It was even better since Natalie went out of town with her cousin to visit family.

"So have you hit her up?" James asked, taking me out of my thoughts.

"Hit who up? Nat?"

James tossed me a "negro, you know" look. I chuckled and shook my head.

"What are you waiting for? She may be over there thinking about you." He put his hand over his chest before smacking his lips, "Ohhh girl, Rashad is so fine," he said with a high pitched voice.

"Man, whatever," I said with a laugh. "I told you that she had a ring on her finger. Brooke isn't checking for me. Plus she was acting strange that day. First she was hella dry and then next she dropping it low on a brother." I took another swig of my beer and shook my head. "I'm good, bro."

"You do know that some women will buy a ring that looks like an engagement ring?" I raised my eyebrows at him. He put a hand up to me before I could say anything. "My sister used to wear a ring on her wedding finger. She said that was how she kept the undesirables away from her. For the most part it worked for her. So, this could be the same thing with Brooke."

"That sounds like complete b.s. my dude," I said laughing. "Brooke ain't wearing no fake ring to scare off men. I know her."

James laughed and shrugged his shoulders before turning his attention back to the television. In those few moments of silence, I thought about what he said regarding the ring being a decoy. I knew Brooke. She would never do anything like that. It wasn't her style to be fake about anything in her life. It did give me enough false hope to want to reach out to her. I just really wanted to know how she was doing. That's all. There was no harm in wanting to know about her well-being.

"Hey bro! Can you bring me another beer on your way back?" James asked as I got up and started walking to the back of my apartment.

"Nah, I can't you lazy ninja!" I said with a laugh as I made it to my bedroom and closed the door.

I grabbed my laptop off of my desk and sat down on the edge of my bed. I still had her email address from college.

What if she changed it? I thought to myself. It was a real possibility that she could have when we broke up. Chances are she blocked me and my email wouldn't be received anyway. I was stumped at how I could get a message to her. I thought about hitting my brother up to see if he could get her sister to give me her number.

Facebook! The popular social media site has the ability to reconnect people. I logged into my account and entered her name in the search bar.

"Bingo!" I mumbled with a satisfied smile as I clicked on her name to bring up her profile. Of course it was private and I couldn't see everything. That didn't stop me from clicking on her photos to see what was public. The first picture of was of her and who I assumed was her dude.

Since when did she like yellow guys? I bet those are color contacts in his eyes. Gay.

"Bing!"

The sound came from my computer. It was alerting me that someone, that someone being Natalie, wanted to chat. I ignored the notification and proceeded to compose my message to Brooke. Once I was done typing the message, I read it over to make sure it made sense. I tried to keep it causal and not come off as if I was trying to sweat her. If I believed in the power of prayer I would have prayed before I sent the message, but prayer hasn't worked in my life.

"Here goes nothing," I said as I sent the message.

Chapter 11

Brooke

I set the platter of fruit down on the coffee table as I sat down next to Dee on the couch. We were preparing to do our version of Netflix and chill. Good thing I was already pregnant and didn't run the risk of getting pregnant again.

I still hadn't shared with him the news. I was almost 12 weeks. I actually had my first appointment with Patrice a couple of weeks ago to check on the baby. I felt instantly connected to the little bean growing inside of me.

Part of the reason I didn't want to tell Dee was because I knew that he would want to get married right away. This baby bonded me to him forever. Forever. Something I didn't know if I wanted; especially after seeing Rashad a couple of months ago.

I couldn't get him out of my mind. I had vivid dreams of making love to him. I could literally feel every kiss, every touch, and every time he would enter me. When that happened I would wake up in a sweat and look around. Dee told me one time I was moaning in my sleep. Of course, he thought it was because of something he did before we went to bed. I let him have that one. There was absolutely no way I was going to tell him that I was having sexual dreams about my first love.

"What do you want to watch?" Dee asked as he flipped through the options on Netflix.

"After the week I had, I need something that will have me laughing. This rotation is kicking my butt," I said with a laugh.

He didn't respond but kept flipping through the options. It was almost as if he was going through the motions but it was obvious he had something on his mind. If I had to guess, it had to do with Sheba's stupid behind. She had been withholding Justice from him for over a month. She claimed she was upset that he wouldn't watch Justice for her when she wanted to go to the salon.

"You still mad about Sheba?" I asked. "I told you that you should take her to court and get custody of him."

He still didn't respond.

"Babe?"

He turned to look at me. "I got something to show you." He got up and walked over to his overnight bag.

"Ohhh, surprise!" I exclaimed with a clap of my hands. I had no idea how much of a surprise I was in for. As I waited, I decided to log in to my Facebook account. It had been a couple of days since I had logged on. As soon as I did I saw that I had a couple of inbox messages waiting for me. One of the messages was from my baby sister, Brittany, letting me know that she wanted to come visit for Labor Day weekend. The other message was from Rashad. I felt my mouth go dry. I pondered if I should open it but before I could, Dee walked back to the couch carrying a plastic bag.

I looked up at him with a smile. The gesture was not returned. He remained stoic as he dumped the contents of the bag on to the couch next to me. My phone slipped out of my hand. I felt the bile rise up inside of my mouth. I swallowed hard to keep myself from throwing up. I began to take noticeable deep breaths to help prevent the impending panic attack.

"I can explain, Dee," I said as I reached for his hand. He took a step back and moved to the love seat.

I stared down at the empty pregnancy boxes. There were three. I kept the actual tests in my nightstand drawer. I'm not sure why I was holding on to them. I think it was part of my denial.

"Well," he began quietly. "Are you still pregnant?"

I nodded my head as tears began to fall from my eyes. I heard him sigh deeply.

"I was going to say something. I just didn't know how. How did you…" my voice trailed off.

"I found them that day you were at the Greek picnic. I was taking the trash out and they were right there. No tests. Just empty boxes. I waited for you to tell me. And I waited. But you never said anything. You just kept living life. So I thought you had an abortion and you weren't going to ever tell me."

"I thought about getting an abortion, but I couldn't do that. I tried to tell-"

"You didn't try to tell me shit, Brooke!" he exploded at me. He was big mad. He never cursed at me or even around me, so I knew that he was upset.

"God, why wouldn't you tell me?" he continued.

"I wasn't sure what I was going to do," I said with my head down. I tried to keep my focus on my hands; which were starting to shake with anxiety.

He got up off the couch, grabbed his keys, and started towards to the front door. I hopped off the couch and quickly moved in front of the door to block him from leaving.

"Please don't go, Dee. Let me explain everything!" I pleaded with him. I attempted to reach for his free hand but he stepped back. His eyes told me that I needed to get out of the way, but I stood in front him defiantly. I took a step toward him. He didn't move.

"I…" my voice trailed off as I tried to regain my composure. I sighed deeply and took another step toward him. There was no longer any space between the two of us. He kept his focus on the front door. I looked up at him and with my hands gently guided his face down to look at me. This time he didn't resist me. "I'm sorry, baby. I was scared. I was concerned with finishing school. I have a year left in medical school and having a baby will complicate things. I thought if I had an abortion my life wouldn't be complicated, but I knew that it was wrong and it was selfish. This baby doesn't deserve to die because of the decision I made. I have enough things to ask God for forgiveness for. Killing an innocent child in order for me to finish medical school is not something I want to add."

A single tear fell from his eyes. I hadn't noticed that I was crying until he gently wiped away a runaway tear from my face. He gently caressed my face as he leaned forward to touch my forehead with his. He then kissed me on the forehead and began walking toward the front door. I didn't turn around.

"I don't get it, Brooke. I love you so much," he started. "I think we need some space to think about everything. I'll call you."

With that, he walked out the door. I stood where he left me and continued to weep.

Chapter 12

Brooke

Seven days. It had been seven whole days and counting since I had last physically saw and spoken to Dee. We've never gone 24 hours without speaking to each other and never two days without seeing one another. Other than medical school and my family, he has been the only other constant person in my life. Ever since he confronted me about being pregnant, he's stayed away from me. He would only text me to see how I was doing. He kept his messages short and to the point. One time I tried to engage him in conversation, but I fell asleep awaiting his response.

This was a side of Dee I've never experienced. In our three years of dating, I've never seen him get as angry as he was last week. Not even at Sheba and she did some off the wall things to him. He always kept his cool. I was going crazy not talking to him, which confused the mess out of me.

Before I got pregnant, I was confused about the future of our relationship. I was praying that God would show me a sign that I needed to move on from him. I struggled with telling him that I no longer wanted to have sex. However, here I sat in the doctor's lounge trying to decide if I should call him or not. This was my on-call weekend for my pediatric rotation. I had already completed my rounds for the night and I planned on staying the night at the hospital in the event I got a call. It was easier for me to stay the night than to drive from my house in Duluth.

I decided to text him. While I waited for him to respond, I checked my Facebook. When I logged on, I remembered that I had a message from Rashad in my inbox. I clicked on my messages to read what he said.

Brooke,

It's been a while. I hope that you're doing well. I know we didn't get a chance to talk at the picnic, but I wanted to see how you were doing. Parker told me that you're in medical school at Emory. If the medical program is anything like the law program, then I know you're busy… you don't have to respond. Just wanted to drop you a line.

Shad

I read the message at least ten more times before closing out of the app without responding. His message was simple, but it felt like a loaded gun. I debated on responding. I knew that if I did, that I was going to be opening up Pandora's box, but it would be rude of me not to respond.

Rashad,

It's nice to hear from you. I'm doing well. I hope all is well with you. Your assumption would be correct about my schedule being busy, but I had a little time to respond.

Brooke

I read my message one more time to ensure that I kept it cordial. The last thing I needed to do was open up the door to my past, but it flew open when I saw him at the picnic. I noticed that I still hadn't received a response back from Dee. Maybe he was sleeping. It was going on midnight and he usually went to bed early. I decided to call him in hopes he would answer his phone.

"Brooke," he answered groggily.

I breathed a silent sigh of relief before answering. "Hi, baby."

"What's up? Are you okay? Is the baby okay?"

"Yes, we're fine. I just haven't heard your voice and I missed you."

I heard him rumble in the background. I assumed he was sitting up in the bed. I didn't say anything, but waited for him to say something. It felt like an eternity before he spoke again.

He sighed. "I miss you too, Brooke. I'm just still hurt and not ready to talk to you. I love you. God, I love you so much. But I can't figure out why you wouldn't tell me you were carrying my seed. It makes no sense."

It was my turn not to respond. I didn't know what to say. There was nothing I could say that would make sense. I guess I took too long to respond because I heard him clear his throat.

"I'm sorry, Dee. I can't give you a reason that would make any sense."

"You know what I go through with Sheba. How she manipulates and keeps my son away from me. The fact that you weren't going to tell me about the baby is crazy. You of all people know my situation. The shit is foul, Brooke."

Again, I had nothing for him. Instead I felt warm water running down my face. I wiped my nose with the back of my hand and closed my eyes. I wish I could turn back the hands of time. I didn't want to lose him this way.

"Look," he started, "I love you, that will never change. I still need some time. I'm not saying we're breaking up or anything like that. Just need to digest everything."

"Okay and I love you, too," I sniffled.

"I'll call you. Soon. Aight."

I nodded my head but realized he could not see me. "Okay." I managed to say through tears.

There was silence again, but this time he disconnected the call. I looked at my phone in disbelief. I couldn't believe the direction my relationship was heading. As I held my phone, I received an alert from Facebook informing me that I had a new message. I went in my inbox and I saw that it was from Rashad.

I'm surprised you responded. Lol. Why you up so late?

I felt my heart skip a beat. I knew responding to him was a bad idea. I was flooded with a thousand emotions. Familiar emotions that I knew were wrong given the circumstances, but in that moment I didn't care. My heart was wounded and I needed peace. Even if that peace came at a price. Rashad's message temporarily dismissed my drama with Dee. I responded without any more hesitation.

Lol! I am a 3rd year medical student. Sleep left me a long time ago. I'm actually on call tonight. I'm about to go to sleep in a few. I plan to go to church on tomorrow morning. Why you still up?

While I waited for his response, I took off my shoes and laid in the bed provided in the doctor's lounge. My alert went off.

Yeah, I guess that would keep you up all night. You on call often? I just got in. What church you go to?

Rashad and I chatted online for another hour or so until I got paged to see about a patient. The conversation had remained lighthearted and friendly. A part of me felt guilty for having a conversation with him. If Rashad had been any other male, I wouldn't have felt guilty. I was going into a field that was heavily dominated by men. The conversations I had with them were always platonic. However, this conversation was different. Not only was he my ex, but I still had feelings for him. Feelings that never died when we broke up in college.

The next morning in church, I was fighting to keep my eyes open. The patient I saw last night took a little longer to stabilize than anticipated. By the time I got them stable it was almost six in the morning. Thankfully, I brought clothes with me for church and opted to go to the early morning service.

Pastor Kevin, the senior pastor's brother, came up as the choir finished their last selection. He stood at the podium and lifted his hands up. It seemed as if the entire church was under a spell. The spirit of God was definitely moving after that riveting rendition of the John P. Kee classic, "Standing in the Need."

"Y'all be seated in the house of God today," Pastor Kevin said as he wiped sweat away from his brow. In a quizzically tone he asked, "How many of us are in need of prayer?"

One lady in the church yelled out, "Me, oh Lord!"

"Oftentimes, we forget that we have a secret weapon right at our fingertips. We forget that we have the privilege of going to our Heavenly Father in prayer. We seem to only pray when life is beating us down. But how many of you know that you should pray at all times?"

"Preach Doc," a man yelled out.

"We have forgotten that there is power in our prayers. We have forgotten that prayer changes things. You see, when we don't pray, we end up taking the driver's seat in our lives. We feel as if we can handle everything. It's as if we are running the show. You remember what happened when Sarah took matters into her own hands? Had she waited on God…Had she talked to God while waiting on his promise, she could have avoided all the baby mama drama!"

"Watch out now!" the same man called out.

"You got to pray. It's your life line. It's time for the people of God to humble themselves before Him. I encourage you today to pray. If you have an ex trying to come back in your life. Pray about it. If you are doing great. Pray about it. Pray about everything. Stop waiting and pray. If you need prayer today, I encourage you to step out and come to the altar."

I immediately made my way to the altar while he was still talking. I heard people clapping as I walked. With tears streaming down my face, I kneeled before the altar and bowed my head. I had one prayer request. I needed God not to allow me to fall in love with Rashad again.

Later that evening, I was at home trying to figure out what to eat. Since becoming pregnant I craved carbs and by carbs I mean lots of bread. It didn't matter the type of bread either. Bread was the only thing that seemed to settle my stomach. As I was pondering what bread to eat, my house phone rang. I walked over to the kitchen counter where I kept the cordless phone.

"Hi Mama," I said, excitedly.

"Hey BJ. What are you up too?" she asked.

I wrinkled my face when I heard her call me BJ. I loathed that nickname because it sounded masculine, but all of my family called me BJ. Rumor has it that I was going to be named after my father because my parents were told that I was a boy. I can imagine how surprised they must have been when the doctor announced I was a girl.

"Ma, you know I don't like to be called BJ," I said, pretending to be exasperated.

She laughed. "I know honey, but you will always be BJ to me. You look just like your father. Well, not so much anymore. You get what I mean, girl."

"Yes, I do." I laughed. "So what are you and Daddy up to? Did you guys have a good time in Belize?"

"Oh, we had a marvelous time. However, I've been feeling a little under the weather since we got back."

"You didn't get bit or anything like that, did you?"

"I think a mosquito could've gotten me, but nothing serious. I'm probably just tired from all of the traveling. I only took a couple of days off before heading back to work."

"Sounds like you need some rest. Are you going to be able to do so this weekend?"

"I should. Brittany is driving up this weekend from Houston, but you know she'll be visiting her little friends. We hardly see her when she comes home from school."

"She hit me up on Facebook and wanted to fly here for Labor Day weekend. I was like okay, but I'm not sure how she plans on getting here. I ain't got no money."

My mother laughed but then started to cough violently.

"You okay, Ma?" I said concerned.

She cleared her throat and what sounded like a sip of water.

"Yeah, I'm fine. It felt like something got caught in my throat. But anyway, how are you and Dee doing? Are you going to bring him to Texas this year for the holiday?"

"I'm not sure, Ma. He's a little upset with me right now. I hope he'll come home with me though."

"Is that what you want, BJ?'

Her question threw me for a loop. I wasn't sure what she was implying. I started to feel a little light headed, so I sat down at one of the chairs in my dining room.

"Ma, I'm not sure what you mean. Why wouldn't I want him to come home with me? He's been coming home for Christmas for two years now."

"Brooke, I know you're pregnant. I also know that you aren't as into Donovan as you were in the beginning of your relationship. Oh and I know that you saw Rashad at the Greek Picnic. Did I miss anything?"

I was at a loss of words. The only thing I shared with her was the engagement. There was no way I could trust Bree to keep her mouth shut. But how did she know I was pregnant?

As if she could hear my thoughts, "I know my child. I knew you were expecting when we came to visit. A mother knows these things. But your sister told me about Rashad."

"Oh," was all I could manage.

"As for your relationship with Donovan… well… I've always liked him, but I knew you were settling. Don't get me wrong, he is a nice, young man. But he has a crazy baby mama and he's still in community college. He has a dead end job and he doesn't seem to have any life goals. But you love him and have chosen to stay with him this long. So now you're pregnant with his child, engaged and still don't know if you want to be with him for the rest of your life. But this child will bind you two together…"

"I know Mama. I love him, but then I saw Rashad and he recently reached out to me. If I wasn't confused before, I am now. I knew I should've left Dee after finding out about Justice and what went down with Sheba during that time. But he treats me so well, Mama. I don't know what I'm going to do…"

"Pray baby."

"Funny… that's what Pastor Kevin preached about today. He came and spoke at the main campus."

"Well, God is trying to tell you something. I don't know the last time you two chatted, but keep on praying until you hear from Him."

"Okay, Ma. I will. Well, let me go. I need to feed your grandchild. Oh and did you tell Daddy I was pregnant?"

"Oh, gosh no!" she laughed. "I'm going to let you handle that one, BJ."

"Geez, thanks Mama!" I laughed through my tears.

"Alright, baby. Let me go. I need to lay it down and get ready for the work week. I love you."

"I love you, too, Ma."

After I hung up with my mother, I went to lay down in my bed. This weekend had officially drained me of any emotions. The little I still had were left on the altar at church this morning. I felt the need to pray again and this time to be specific in what I was seeking from God.

"Lord, I come to You with a humble heart. I thank You for waking me up this morning and for giving me life. I thank You for abundant life. I thank You for not giving up on me, even when I wanted to give up on myself. Father, I ask that You would forgive me of all of my sins. I know that I've messed up and I've sinned. Please remove those things that are not like You and create in me a new heart.

God, as You know, I'm pregnant by Dee. I love him so much, God. I really do. But I don't know if he is the one I should be with for the rest of my life. Then there is Rashad. That day when I saw him everything came rushing back. Then yesterday when he reached out to me, I finally realized I still love him. But God, he hurt me so bad. He became his father and didn't even realize it. I have this baby and Rashad is with Natalie. Lord, I don't know what I want from either man at this time. But what I want from You is peace of mind and heart. I don't know what will happen between Dee and me, but whatever happens let it be Your will. Just don't let me do anything stupid as it concerns Rashad, because I sense that our paths will cross again. Amen."

Chapter 13

Rashad

The Starbucks on campus was always live, especially during midterms and finals. It wasn't uncommon to see jittery freshmen and sleep deprived graduate students huddled in a corner. This midterm season proved no different. Thankfully, being in my last year of law school, those days were long gone.

Today I was meeting with Denise to go over some final details for our mock trial competition, that was rapidly approaching in the coming weeks. It was my suggestion to meet in a neutral place to keep myself from temptation. Although, that has never stopped me before from going after what I want.

Denise was sitting across from me wearing her hair up in a neat bun. She was dressed in a pair of Active Ego leggings and top. Even in workout clothes, she was still fine and I was still tempted to touch her in sinful ways.

"I think the one good thing about this competition is that we don't have to travel this year," she said, peering over her laptop.

I chewed my bagel and nodded my head in agreement at her statement.

"Yeah. Last year was crazy traveling down to Jacksonville. Be nice if they would reimburse us for these competitions; especially since we win," I said.

"I know right. So the only other thing I think we need to do is go over the witness statements. Oh and maybe work on Jessica's closing argument."

"Her closing is pretty weak. I'm not sure she understands how the closing works, but I think that has to do with her being a 2L."

"You're prob-" she stopped talking mid-sentence. As I prepared to turn around to see what had her attention, I felt a hand touch my shoulder. I knew who it was without having to completely turn around.

"Hi, baby. Do you mind if I sit?"

Natalie didn't wait for permission as she pulled out the chair next to me. Denise smirked and shook her head in disbelief. I wanted to get up and walk away from the table. I admit that Natalie and I were in a good place at the moment. Matter of fact, we hadn't argued since she returned from her vacation. But I didn't know why she was here now.

When we spoke earlier, I told her that I would be busy during the morning prepping for the mock trial and that we would get together later in the day. I was trying to remember if I told her that I was going be alone with Denise.

"I didn't know I would run into you this morning," Natalie said as she took a sip of her drink.

Denise got up and placed her shades on top of her head.

"Oh, Denise! I didn't mean to run you away." Natalie feigned ignorance.

"Bitch please," Denise whispered. She rolled her eyes and sighed as she proceeded to gather her things. "I'm going to run, Rashad. I'll call you later to see when we want to hold these final practices."

With that she walked off without further acknowledging Natalie. I looked over at Natalie who was sitting with a smug look on her face. I couldn't figure this girl out. One minute she was cool as a cucumber but then there were times like this when I wasn't sure if she was missing a few screws in the head.

It was as if she figured out where I was going to be at and made it a point to show up. I know that it sounded crazy but this was becoming more normal for her. First, it was at the parking deck. I'm almost sure I saw a girl that looked like her at the sports bar that night Denise tried to get at me, but I dismissed that as quickly as I thought it. She couldn't be that crazy.

"So what's up, Nat?" I asked as I calmly took a swig of my coffee.

She didn't respond immediately. Her eyes were fixated on the door Denise walked out of. I cleared my throat loudly to get her attention. She slowly turned her head towards me. The smirk from earlier was replaced with an ice cold glare.

In a chilling tone she asked, "Do you know how much I love you?"

Instead of responding, I took another sip of my coffee. I wasn't sure how to respond to her. Something told me to walk away before things escalated. The last thing I needed was to have a public blow up. Against my better judgement I decided to entertain the conversation.

"Enlighten me," I said with an even tone.

"More than you will ever know. Please don't make me have to fuck you or a bitch up over you. Because I will and I won't think twice about it. Especially if I sense I'm being disrespected. I'm not to be played with Rashad. You better ask somebody. That hoe has no more times to come for you like that."

I was speechless. This chick was crazy for real. I laughed and took another sip of my coffee before standing up. She stood up with me as if she dared me to walk out. I gently grabbed her hand and leaned over to whisper something in her ear.

"I'm going to say this once. I'm not to be played with either. Don't let the smoothness fool you. Come by my house today and get your shit. We are done."

I kissed her on the cheek for effect and left her there looking stupid.

When I made it to my car I sat in it and tried to process what took place with Natalie. I punched the steering wheel twice and yelled out a few expletives. A few I knew my mother would immediately wash my mouth out with soap for. I was pissed that she had finally pulled me down to her level. I wanted to choke her! Since I couldn't and get away with it, I had to find another way to release this anger. I grabbed my phone from my pocket and sent out a text. A few minutes later, I got the response I needed and headed in the direction of my stress reliever.

The Johns Creek area had to be one of the many exclusive areas in the Atlanta metro. It boasted of massive homes that housed celebrities and pro football players. It was nothing to see one of the ladies from reality television in the grocery store. It was also where Denise lived at home with her parents.

When we first started dating she told me stayed in the guest house on her parent's property. Her guest house was a three bedroom, two bathroom house. It would be considered an upgraded starter home. She even had a separate drive way to get to her residence.

I parked my car next to her Mercedes E class. I hadn't been to Denise's place since we had broken up before our second year of law school. Although we remained cordial after the break up, there was still an undeniable attraction. If I was honest, Denise came close to Brooke, but she wasn't Brooke and never would be. The thought of Brooke almost caused me to turn around from Denise's house. For a brief moment I felt as if I was getting ready to cheat on Brooke. She and I had been communicating every other day since I had reached out to her on Facebook. It was like before we started dating in high school. Having her back in my life, even if it may be short lived, felt as is if I had my best friend back.

I shook the thoughts of Brooke off and made my way to Denise's door. Her hair was wet and her face was fresh. She wore a short, purple satin robe with matching house shoes. She kissed me on the lips before moving out of the way to let me in the door.

"Do you want anything to drink?" she asked as she took my jacket to hang in the closet.

"Nah, I'm good. I see you got the blunt rolled already," I said as I reached the living room and sat on the couch.

"From your text I sensed you could use a little pick me up."

She joined me on the couch where I had already started taking my first hit. It had been a few months since I last smoked. Smoking was a habit I picked up during my first year of law school. Matter of fact, I started smoking with Denise. I remember being surprised that a woman of her pedigree smoked weed. She referred to it as her anxiety medication.

"You have no idea," I said as I took another drag before passing it to her.

"You date Natalie. I'm surprised you don't need anything stronger."

"Let's not talk about her. I didn't come here to talk about her."

"Fine," she said, throwing up her hands in fake surrender. "I don't like your crazy ass girlfriend anyway, so we definitely don't have to talk about her."

I didn't respond. Instead I took another hit of the blunt and began flipping through the channels. Denise was starting to ruin my high and irritate me. As if sensing my irritation, she began to rub my manhood. I acted as if I wasn't fazed by her touch, but my lower head failed me. As soon as she got me hard, she straddled me and started tonguing me down. I matched her passion as I began to rub my hands across her ass. She abruptly stopped kissing me and sat up on my lap.

"I'm going to go freshen up. Why don't you come join me in the room?"

She winked and walked toward her bedroom. As I was getting up, my phone vibrated in my pocket. It was a text from Brooke. I took the plunge a few nights ago and gave her my number. I was surprised she sent a text back to ensure I had her number as well.

Hey you. What you up to?

Her text was enough to stop me in my tracks. I felt myself sober up, no longer interested in smashing Denise. I grabbed my stuff and proceeded to leave. I figured I would text Denise later saying something came up.

"So you were just going to leave and not say anything?"

I didn't hear Denise come out of her room. She stood in the living room with her arms folded across her chest. Her green eyes told me she was pissed, but more hurt by my actions. Under different circumstances I would have showed compassion, but at this moment I didn't give a damn.

"Yeah, my bad. Something came up and I need to go take care it. I was going to call you later."

She twisted her face. "Rashad, you must think I'm some kind of fool."

I threw my hand up and turned back to the front door. "Man, whatever. I don't got time for this. I'll hit you later. Aight."

I opened the door and walked to my car. Before I made it inside my car, Denise yelled my name out from her front door. I turned around and looked at her. She took a deep breath and wiped at her face. With venom dripping in her voice she yelled, "Hey, the next time you trolling for ass because your bitch hurt your feelings, do me a favor? Don't call me."

With that she slammed her door shut. I wasn't sure if her parents heard her or not. I didn't care. I got in my car and started it up. Before I pulled off, I responded back to Brooke.

Hey. Nothing much. What's up with you?

Nothing. I'm getting ready to leave my rotation and you crossed my mind. Just wanted to check in on you. I hope you had a great day.

Her response made me smile. I put my phone down and proceeded to head out of Denise's neighborhood. I had been so deep in thought about Brooke that I hadn't seen the car following me out the neighborhood.

Chapter 14

Rashad

The day of the mock trial competition had arrived. The month leading up to it proved to be awkward between Denise and me. The tension between us was noticeable. Prior to the incident at her house, she and I were trial partners. Clearly that wasn't going to work if she refused to speak to me. She ended up informing the coach that she needed to switch partners or she would quit the team. Being that she was one of the best mock trial members, her wish was granted. She ended up partnering with James and I with Jessica. I could tell that Jessica wasn't going to be a litigator and if we made it through the next round, it would be pure luck.

I still hadn't spoken to Natalie since the Starbucks incident. She called or texted me once a week. I never answered her phone calls. Instead I would text to ask when she was coming to get her stuff. Once I realized she wasn't coming to get her stuff, I brought her stuff with me to school. In the two years we were dating, there was never a day I didn't see her at least once at school. But now, I never saw her. I even tried to give her stuff to Tori, but Tori said they weren't speaking to one another. When I probed into what happened. She, like everyone else, said that Natalie was crazy. Her exact words were "That chick is crazy and I had to move out."

"Hi, baby."

I turned around to see Natalie standing in front of me. I was outside of a conference room in the Georgia World Congress Center, waiting to go in to start my competition. For a split second a feeling of paranoia came over me. I had to admit she looked good. Her long hair was pulled up into a neat bun, similar to how Denise wore her hair at Starbucks. She wore a pair of skinny jeans so tight I knew she wasn't wearing any panties. She completed her look with a red short sleeve blouse and a cream camisole underneath. Surprisingly, she wore a pair of red suede flats.

Before I responded to Natalie, I stuck my head in the conference room to let Jessica know that I was going to take a quick walk before the competition got started. I turned back to Natalie and gently grabbed her by her arm. The last thing I needed was for her to act a fool.

Once outside I released Natalie's arm. Before I spoke I saw Denise walk up. She looked over at where we were standing and shook her head in disgust.

"What the hell are you doing here?" I spat as soon as we were alone.

She shook her head before responding, "Tsk tsk. I'm here to support my man." She reached up and attempted to stroke my face. I whipped my head back and took a couple of steps back. She clapped her hands and busted out laughing. I was dumbfounded. She abruptly stopped laughing and closed the gap between us.

"I know you didn't think you could end the relationship between us. Look I know you're upset by what I said. I was wrong, but baby I love you and we're going to work through this together."

"You're crazy, Natalie."

She shrugged her shoulders and left me standing outside. I watched her walk inside the building as if she owned the world. I observed her speak to a few classmates. I looked down at my watch and saw that I had less than fifteen minutes to get prepared for my competition. Natalie had me rattled. I didn't know how I was going to get rid of her but after today I knew that I had to handle her carefully. Otherwise I could be in a real live fatal attraction situation...If I wasn't already.

"Here is to another successful competition. We are the best future litigators here and today proved that! Cheers!" our mock trial professor said, raising his glass of wine.

"Cheers!" we all exclaimed.

The mock trial competition proved to be successful. Despite Natalie's presence, I was able to stay focused. After it was over, the entire team headed over to the Cheesecake Factory at Perimeter Mall. During the celebration, Denise and I made subtle eye contact. I could see that she was still upset, but her demeanor seemed off. I could tell that she had something on her mind. I sent her text asking if she wanted to go outside and talk. She agreed to step outside with me.

"Your bitch and I had a conversation today," she said as soon as we stepped outside.

I was taken off guard by her statement. Because we were working with different partners, I didn't see her until the end of the competition. I wondered when Natalie had time to speak to her.

As if reading my mind she said, "She had the nerve to corner me in the bathroom during one of the breaks."

"Wow."

"Wow? Really Rashad?"

"I mean what do you want me to say? How would I know she was going to corner you? She and I broke up."

"Oh. Well, she clearly didn't get the memo. She proceeded to tell me to stay away from you. That you were her man and that she will beat my ass if she sees me ever talking to you. I started to punch her in her mouth but Jessica came in the bathroom and broke us up."

"Damn, Denise. I'm really sorry. I can't believe she did that. I mean I can talk to her, if it would make you feel better." I attempted to grab her hand, but she stepped back from my reach.

"Don't Rashad. What you can do for me, is stay the hell away from me. I can't deal with this type of drama. I'm not going to be threatened. That trick had the nerve to tell me that she knew where I lived at and that she would set my house on fire."

I wrinkled my face. How would Natalie know where Denise lived? None of this was making sense. When I didn't respond, Denise walked back into the restaurant. I stood outside for a minute trying to process the last statement Denise made.

We were all standing outside waiting for the valet to bring our vehicles. My mind was still processing the conversation with Denise. I wanted to tell James about what happened, but I figured I would wait.

As James and I stood around talking, there was a loud scream. We turned to the direction of the scream and saw Denise running to her car as the valet ran behind her. James and I took off after them to see what happened. Once at Denise's car, we noticed that three of her tires had been slashed and the word BITCH had been scratched in capital letters across the hood of her car.

She turned to me with tears in her eyes and started walking towards me. Once she reached me, Denise reached up and slapped the shit out of me. I rubbed my cheek where she slapped me.

"I'm sorry, Denise. I don't know what else to say."

"Whatever Rashad. You and I know why she did this. Just please stay far, and I do mean far, away from me," she said through tears. With that she turned away and pulled out her phone.

"Come on, man. Let's go," James said, turning back to head to the front of the restaurant.

I stared at Denise. I didn't want to leave her at that moment. At least not until I knew that everything was going to be alright. I knew she didn't want me near her or want my help. As I followed James back to the front of the restaurant my phone vibrated. I pulled it out and saw Parker calling me.

"What's up?" I answered.

"You busy man?" he said with a sense of urgency in his voice.

"Nah, I'm good. What's wrong with you?"

"Man, you need to make it a point to get back home. There's some weird stuff going on with Mom and Dad."

"That's not new, Park."

"Nah, Mama is walking around here crying. Her and Dad have been getting into it. I thought the other night he was going to hit her."

I couldn't believe what I was hearing. It was as if my brother was speaking a foreign language. This day had to be the worst day ever. It didn't matter how my competition went, because everything happening to me and around me was overshadowing my win.

"Did you hear what I said?" Parker asked, taking me away from my thoughts.

"Huh. Nah, what did you say Park?"

"I just got a text from Bree about their mom. You need to get here ASAP."

"What happened to their mom?"

"Not sure yet, but she's in the hospital."

Chapter 15

Brooke

"She's going to be beautiful," I thought as I watched the ultrasound screen. Patrice was finishing my first trimester screen at her office. It was too early to tell the sex of the baby, but I believed in my heart that I was having a girl.

"Alright hun. It looks like everything is checking out so far. We will determine the sex when you come back for your anatomy scan," Patrice said as she rolled away to type some information in the computer.

"That feels like an entirety."

"It is. I hope you have a girl so that our girls can play together."

"I know right. I've already claimed that I'm having a girl."

She laughed and handed me a paper towel to wipe off the gel used during the ultrasound. I was happy that Patrice decided to keep her baby and workout her marriage with her husband. It seemed that the months of intensive marriage counseling and individual counseling for her finally paid off. She was more pleasant to be around and her faith in God had grown.

"So where are you going after this? You have the dinner with Dee tonight, right?"

"Yeah, I do, but I'm going to see Marion to get my hair done first."

"Tell him I need to come see him, but I may go ahead and get my hair braided by Catherine. I'm so over fooling with my hair and this sew in is getting on my nerves!"

"I had lunch with Catherine and Yvonne last week. They are so crazy, but I will tell Marion you will call him to make an appointment. I'm sure he would be happy to see you and hear about everything."

"I know girl. Well, go up front and make an appointment for next month. I hope your dinner with Dee goes well, sis." Patrice said hugging me as she walked me out to the hallway.

"Pray for me girl." I laughed.

"You don't know how much I needed this," I said as Marion massaged my scalp at the shampoo bowl.

I'm not sure how stylists learn how to massage scalps well. I assume there is a special class that teaches them. Marion was literally rubbing all my struggles away with his scalp massage. I lay with my hands across my small baby bump with my eyes closed. I must've fell asleep because Marion was tapping my shoulder and attempting to lift my head up from the shampoo bowl.

"Girl, you were starting to snore," he said with a slight chuckle.

I yawned and stretched my arms above my head. "My bad. I'm so tired. This is the first day I've had to myself."

"I bet. What rotation are you doing now?"

"Surgery. I'm so over it already."

Marion placed a shower cap on my head and guided me over to one of the hair dryers. He set the timer for 15 minutes. As I sat under the dryer I sent a text to Dee to confirm our dinner date and another text to check on Rashad. As I waited for a response, I scrolled through my various social media sites.

I still couldn't believe Rashad and I had reconnected after all of these years. We still haven't had a talk about our break up in college. I'm not sure why he didn't bring it up, but I still got angry when I thought about the way he did it. I knew that I needed to forgive him. I had to forgive him in order to be fully free. However, with us talking again I feared that forgiveness would allow me to become vulnerable to him again. It was bad enough that we spoke as if we never stopped talking. It reminded me of when we were kids and we would sit outside on my parents' porch talking into the wee hours. He was my best friend. The best friend that I loved and I wanted to spend forever with.

I looked down at my phone as it vibrated. I received messages from both Rashad and Dee. The message from Rashad made me smile. Every message from Rashad made me smile. The message from Dee caused me to frown and roll my eyes. I placed my phone back in my purse and lifted the hood of the dryer up. I walked over to Marion's styling chair and sat down. Marion came over to the chair a few minutes later after he placed another client under the dryer.

"Do you think you can trim my ends? They are starting to look a little ragged," I said as he parted my hair into sections before preparing to blow dry it.

"Yeah, I will. So what time is your date with Dee tonight?"

I held up seven fingers to indicate the time of the date. I never quite understood why stylists attempted to have full blown conversations with you while using a loud blow dryer. It seemed counterproductive when attempting to have a conversation. Marion must have sensed my agitation and didn't speak again until he completed drying my hair.

"How are you two doing?" he asked as he began to clip my ends.

I sighed, "We doing."

"It's like that?"

"Yup. I'm surprised that we're going out for dinner. He still isn't really talking to me, so I'm not sure how well this dinner is going to go."

"Is he still upset about you not telling him about the baby?"

"Yeah. I mean I get it, but at what point do you get over it? Like he knows now and I'm keeping the baby."

"Brooke, you know us men are funny when we get hurt. My wife and I have had our fair share of issues. When I was younger I would hold things against her for days. It would be petty shit, too, but I wanted to be right in the situation and I needed for her to feel hurt."

I didn't say anything. Marion stopped cutting my hair and spun the chair around to face him directly.

"Look, Dee needs to grow up. I've been married for almost 20 years. I married my wife young. I was still a knucklehead and it wasn't until my wife left me for a year that I got it together. We had only been married three or so years, but I was tripping out on her. She had a co-worker that attempted to get at her. She turned down the advances but I was still upset. I felt that she was at fault somehow for this man wanting to talk to her. Now hindsight is 20/20, but I felt threatened as a man. I would make rude comments to her or randomly accuse her of wanting to step out. She got tired of it and left. She stayed with her parents for that year. It took a lot counseling to get us back right, but in that year I grew up. I realized that I didn't want to lose my wife because I had an ego to feed."

"Wow. I didn't know that," I said in disbelief. "You guys are like the picture perfect couple."

Marion let out a hearty laugh. He turned me back around and finished trimming my hair.

"Far from perfect. God has kept us together. We've learned how to weather our storms, but most of all we learned how to communicate. That is what Dee and you need to do. You were wrong for not telling him sooner about the baby. There is no question about that, but he needs to let it go. There are far worse things that you could have done that would warrant him not talking to you. Just seems like you both need to do a little more growing up."

"Yeah, I guess you're right."

As Marion finished up my hair, I sat pondering what tonight would hold for Dee and I. To be honest I wasn't sure if I wanted to reconcile with him. If he could cut me off the way he did, then what makes me think he won't do it again? I hope for the sake of our unborn child that we could make it work and be a family.

"Welcome to Olive Garden. Will it just be the two of you dining with us this evening?" the young female hostess asked as we entered the restaurant.

Dee nodded and we followed the hostess to our table. I'm glad we rode in separate cars because the tension between us was thick. We barely hugged when we saw each other. The only thing that kept me from leaving the restaurant was my excitement about getting ready to eat some breadsticks. There was something about Olive Garden's breadsticks that made my inner fat girl sing a song.

Once seated, the hostess handed us our menus and walked off to the front of the restaurant. Our waitress came over within a couple of minutes after the hostess left. She warmly smiled and spoke to us, as she sat down a few paper napkins and a couple of straws.

"May I get either of something to drink? Perhaps some wine to start your evening off?" she asked.

"No wine for me," I spoke. "However, I will have a sprite and a water."

"Water for me."

"Alright. Do you two need a few more minutes to look over the menu or are you ready to order now?"

"I'm ready to order. Dee are you ready?"

He nodded his head and I proceeded to order my meal. After he ordered, the waitress went to place our orders. The table was silent again. I sighed and looked around the restaurant.

"You look nice," he said after what felt like an eternity.

"Thanks," I said, dryly.

Before things could become any more awkward, the waitress came back with our drink orders and our appetizers. Once she walked away again, I began to wonder if this dinner was a mistake. I didn't plan on spending my free evening looking at him and not talking. I decided to address the pink elephant in the room.

"So, what's up, Dee? What are we doing? I haven't heard from you from real. You act as if I aborted the baby and you found out by chance. I have apologized. I've all but begged for your forgiveness. So before we leave this restaurant we're going to figure out the direction of this relationship."

He didn't respond. Instead he took a sip of his water and another bite of his salad. I wanted to slap the shit out of him. I watched him a few more minutes. With each bite he took I became angrier. Visions of stabbing him with my fork in his eye began to dance in my mind.

Before I could snap he decided to speak.

"I want you, Brooke. I just don't know if I can trust you to tell me things when they happen." I rolled my eyes and took a swig of my drink. He continued, "Don't do that man. I'm saying what you did was foul and it isn't as easy for me to forget about it."

"Dee, I didn't sleep with someone else let's make something real clear. You're not my husband and what I do with my body is absolutely my decision. Whether I kept this baby or not, was solely my decision and never yours."

I could feel people at the tables near me looking over at us. I didn't care. He was starting to piss me off.

"Calm down, Brooke. You're starting to cause a scene."

He reached over to grab my hands but I snatched them back. I peered at him with pure disgust. In this moment, I hated him. I hated myself for allowing this relationship to last as long as it did. Here I am upset with a man I love but I know that I want forever with another man. Gosh, this was too much.

"Look, let's enjoy our dinner. Then we can go home and-" His phone buzzed loudly on the table. We both looked down.

"What the hell does she want?" I asked coldly.

"Its nothing."

He messed with a few buttons on his phone and turned it over so I could no longer view the screen. Before I could protest, our bubbly waitress came to our table and set our food down. Once she ensured we didn't need anything else, we bowed at our heads to say our own individual grace.

Instead of talking, we sat silently and ate our food. I don't know what was running through his mind, but I couldn't help but wonder why Sheba was calling him. Out of the three years we've dated she never called in the evening. She usually made her demands during the day so that by night she would be free to do whatever she had planned. Something wasn't right.

"Can I see your phone?" I boldly inquired.

Dee wrinkled his nose and took another bite of his food before placing his fork down. He looked me straight in my eyes. I matched his gaze. I dared him to deny me access. He sighed deeply. He picked up his phone and attempted to unlock it.

"No. I can unlock it myself."

Again he sighed and passed me his phone. I felt my hand start to shake. I knew that I was asking for trouble, but I needed to know that trouble was in his phone. We've always allowed each other access to our personal accounts. After we had reconciled from his disappearing act in the beginning of our relationship, we made a vow to be open and honest. This was the first time that I had desired to go through his phone and I wanted to do it front of him.

I unlocked his phone and went directly to his text messages. Sheba was the second to the last person he text. I was the first. I opened their messages to one another.

Are you still coming over after you are done with your meeting tonight? Justice will be in the bed by the time you get here.

I didn't read any additional messages. The first one was enough to send my blood boiling. I slammed his phone down on the table. The couple at the table next to us stopped talking and looked our way. Dee sat expressionless. I said nothing for a few minutes. I was trying to find the questions to ask him but I could only think of one.

With chilling calm I asked him, "Are you sleeping with her?"

He looked at me with contempt but said nothing. Instead he smirked, shook his head, and took another bite of his food. Again, thoughts of stabbing him in the eye came to mind. I realized that I was going to have to stoop to a level that only he could understand.

"Let me ask you again. This time I will make sure the people around us can hear. Are. You. Screwing. Your. Baby. Mama?"

It became eerily quiet in the restaurant. I heard someone stifle a laugh. Another person coughed. Our waitress came over to the table.

"Um, ma'am?" she started.

I held my hand up to cut her off. I stood up and grabbed my belongings. The tears were falling fast from my eyes. This time Dee looked sorrowful, but he refused to look my way. I took his silence as an admission of his guilt. The final punch was landed. I was the loser in this fight. Before any more of my dignity was lost in Olive Garden, I headed out of the restaurant.

Once I made it to my car, I sat in the parking lot and cried. I cried and cried until I couldn't muster another tear. All of this stress wasn't be good for my baby. Hell, it wasn't good for me. After composing myself I started my engine and began to drive home. While I was driving I got a call. I answered via the bluetooth of my car.

"Hello," I said.

"Oh my gosh, Brooke! Where have you been?"

I looked at my car radio and saw Breanne's number. I never heard my phone ring because it was on vibrate and buried in my purse. I was driving and not in a position to check my phone to see if I missed her calls.

"Are you okay? What's wrong?"

"You need to get home. Mom is in the hospital."

I almost rear ended the car stopped at the red light. I was still ten minutes from my house. I needed to pull over. Once the light turned green, I turned into the CVS parking lot.

"What do you mean Mom is in the hospital? What happened?"

"I don't know. Daddy called me. He said she passed out at work and she has been out since they arrived at the hospital. Parker is driving me now to the hospital. I will call you when I get more information. Please be by your phone, Brooke."

"I will Bree."

I disconnected the call. What the hell was going on in my life?

Chapter 16

Natalie

I can't believe I got away with it. That'll teach that bitch about messing with my man. Look at her crying over that damn car. She's lucky I didn't do more damage.

I was sitting in a rental car parked in front of the valet station. I could see the drama unfolding in my rearview mirror. I chuckled to myself as I drove off to my apartment. Both Rashad and Denise had been so engrossed with what happened to her car that neither one of them noticed me walking past them to pick up mine.

Before RaShad called himself breaking up with me, I had befriended one of the girls on his mock trial team, June. As our friendship developed, I discovered she lived in the same apartment complex as RaShad. She conveniently lived in the back of his complex and I would have to ride past his building to go to her apartment. It was this discovery that led me to find out that he was messing around with Tori, my now ex-roommate.

As fate would have it, I saw Tori leaving his apartment as I was on my way leaving from June's place. I was actually riding with June to go get my car from the shop. I made a mental note to confront Tori about why in the hell she was at my man's place. I never got the opportunity that day because he and I hung out after class. It was her slick ass comments in the parking garage that confirmed that they had messed around. I wanted to drag her troll behind out of the car, but I played dumb and laughed along with her. Rashad stood there looking stupid. He was trying his best not to poop his pants as Tori talked.

I tried to leave it alone, especially after we made love that night, but then at the Greek picnic he was checking out Brooke. Something about that situation didn't seem right, but I couldn't put my finger on it. I still can't. However, seeing him with Brooke reminded me that I had unfinished business with Tori. It had been a few weeks since I saw her leaving Rashad's place and I waited until our lease was preparing to end to confront her.

"Tori, we need to talk about our living situation."

She rolled her eyes at me and mumbled something under her breath as she turned the television off in the living room. I could tell that she was agitated with me. I didn't give a damn.

"What now, Natalie?" she said with major attitude.

I pretended to be hurt by her tone. "I'm sorry, Tori. Did I do something to offend you that I'm not aware of?"

"No," she sighed. "I'm just having a rough day. I know we need to talk about the apartment. My bad. What's up?"

"Well, I'm not sure this will make your day any better. You see it has been brought to my attention that you have been fucking with my man. Now, I'm not sure if that is acceptable where you come from, but where I come from that will get your ass whooped. Even killed by some. So you

see, you're going to move out. I'll be kind though to give you 72 hours to get out."

She sat on the couch looking like a deer in headlights. Her mouth moved but no words came out. I stared at her with disgust and kept my hand on the butcher knife that laid on the kitchen counter. When she didn't say anything after while, I started walking to my room. As soon as I turned my back I heard her charging down our small apartment hallway.

She grabbed my hair and tried to push me down to the ground. I somehow managed to steady myself enough to be able to push her back into the wall. She still had my hair but after a couple more pushes against the wall, she released it. I ran back into the kitchen and grabbed the knife I had been holding.

"I don't know what the hell your problem is, but I will slice and dice your ass so fast!" I screamed at her.

I ran back into the hallway with the knife. She attempted to run into the bathroom but I pushed her back onto the ground. I quickly got on top of her and held the knife to her throat. Her breathing become hurried as she lay very still under me. We stared at each other. She had tears streaming down her face. I could smell her fear coming through her pores.

"I never meant to mess with him. He came onto me and I-"

I slapped the shit out of her with my free hand. I didn't want to hear her lies. I knew Tori was a hoe. She had more guys coming in and out of our apartment than the trap house. Expect the product was her vagina.

"Just shut up, Tori! I wasn't going to do anything to you. But now if you stay past today, I ..."

She nodded her head. I slowly rose off of her, still holding the knife downward toward her. Once I got up, she shot up and ran to her room. I slammed my bedroom door as I walked into it.

Back at the restaurant, it had been easy to get away with damaging Denise's car. Earlier that day at the competition, I ran into June. She told me that the team was planning on going out to eat afterwards and probably out to some bars. The valet at the restaurant was lacking as usual, and it was easy to slip past them. I had to hold my laughter in as I carved all up and down her pretty car.

I almost got caught when I heard some footsteps heading my way. I quickly ducked behind the car. It was one of the valet drivers running to get the car next to Denise's. I guess he was so caught up that he didn't notice me. I figured that was too close for comfort and I quickly made way back to the restaurant.

I slipped past the valet again, mingled a bit outside with some of the patrons waiting to be seated, and then went to the valet station to get my car. Before I could pull off, I guess one of the valet attendants noticed the damage to Denise's car, because she came out of the restaurant looking crazed. Since the valet wasn't getting other cars, I remained parked at the valet station.

"Checkmate hoe," I said to myself as I smirked. As my grandmother used to say, that will learn her.

Chapter 17

Rashad

I was glad to get away from the drama that had taken place a week ago at the Cheesecake Factory. Denise was never able to prove that Natalie had vandalized her car. The so called security cameras were broken that night and none of the valet saw anything suspicious. But the writing was on the wall, in this case Denise's car, that Natalie did the damage. That night was the last time I spoke with Denise. We didn't have any classes together and with competition being over, we barely saw each other in passing at school.

I still hadn't spoken with Natalie since I saw her at the competition. She sent a few texts but I deleted them as quickly as I received them. Lately my focus had been on my family and Brooke's family. After my call with Parker, I booked a flight back home to Dallas. I then reached out to Brooke to see how she was doing. When I talked to Parker he didn't have all the details about what was going on with their mom, but was on his way taking Bree to the hospital. It would be a few days later before he and I were able to catch up about what was going on with our own parents.

"Man, I don't even know where to begin," Parker started after I answered the phone.

"Is it that bad?" I asked as I moved around my apartment. I was trying to start packing for my flight back home.

"Well, let's just say I've never heard Mom curse and lately she has had a mouth on her. Like from the moment Dad walks in she goes in on him. Dude can say hi and she will just be like, 'Nigga, I know you out there screwing these church hoes."

I had to laugh. I couldn't believe my mother would ever say any of those words. This woman couldn't be paid to curse. The thought of her saying what Parker said was hilarious.

"Dude, you're lying. I'm about fly home for nothing. I could save my frequent flyer miles."

"I know it sounds crazy," he laughed. "But I'm for real. There's something going on. I don't know what, but it's something."

"Let's be honest, if he is sleeping around he's a damn fool. Dallas may be big, but it ain't that big. He's too hungry for power to slip up like that."

"I said the same thing, but you aren't here to see what I see. It's hard to explain, but you'll see when you get here. Speaking of which, did you email your flight info yet?"

"Yeah, I sent it this morning. You think Brooke is going to be there?"

Shoot, I thought. I let that slip out. I hadn't told Parker that Brooke and I had started back communicating. I was trying to wait to see where things were going; if they were going anywhere. I know she hadn't told her sister that we've been talking. I'm not sure her reasoning for not saying anything because they were super close and told each other just about everything. I hoped that Parker didn't read more into my question about Brooke and just assume that I was asking in regards to her mother.

"Yeah. Matter of fact I think she gets in on the same day as you, if I'm not mistaken. I'm supposed to pick her up for Bree. I take it that you two haven't spoken to each other since the Greek picnic?"

I sighed in relief. "Nah, but I figured with her mom being in the hospital she was going to be around."

"Well, you better prepare yourself, because I'm pretty sure you'll see her while you're here."

We continued talking about nothing for a few more minutes. When we got off the phone, I got a text from Natalie asking if she could get the rest of her belongings. I started not to text her back, but against my better judgement I did. I quickly replied she could when I got back from Texas visiting my folks. I sat the phone down and went back to packing for my trip.

"Delta flight 231 with nonstop service to Dallas will be boarding in 15 minutes. Please make sure your boarding pass is ready when you come to the front. This is a full flight and we will need everyone's cooperation in the boarding process. Thank you."

As the flight representative finished giving directions regarding my flight home, I started to clean up my area around me. I had arrived to the airport early and used the quiet time to finish up some work for school. I also grabbed breakfast once I got to the airport as well. For some reason I felt that the Atlanta airport had some of the best restaurants to eat at; that and I was too lazy to get up early enough to eat at home.

As I walked over toward the trashcan, I heard my name being called softly. The voice was familiar and sweet. My face was already smiling when I turned around to see Brooke sitting not too far from the trash. Even without any makeup on she was still a sight to behold. She looked comfortable as she sat her book down and adjusted her purse to place in front of her. Her simple gesture was a welcome invitation to let me know to come sit with her. Without another word, I quickly threw my trash away and retrieved my bags from where I was sitting to sit next to her.

"What are the chances we would be heading back to Dallas on the same day and at the same time?" She said with a smile.

"Kismet," I said as I returned her smile.

She nodded her head in agreement. "Kismet." She repeated softly.

Chapter 18

Brooke

I placed my duffle bag in the back of Rochelle's trunk and got in the passenger seat.

"You all set, girl?" She asked as she pulled away from my apartment complex.

I nodded my head as I sent my sister a text message letting her know that I was on my way to the airport. After I sent the text, I placed my phone back in my purse and closed my eyes. I was tired. I hadn't gotten a decent amount of sleep since my mother was in the hospital. She suffered a seizure which caused her to black out. The doctors were still trying to find the root cause of the seizure but haven't been able to come up with a plausible explanation.

"How are you feeling?" Rochelle asked, snapping me out of my stupor.

I sighed. "Tired. Plain old tried."

"Yeah, I can imagine. I really hope that everything turns out to be okay with your mom."

I didn't respond and looked out the window. I wasn't in the mood for talking. It was too early in the morning and I didn't want to talk about my mom. Thinking about her made me feel helpless. Since she got sick I've started to question my decision to become a doctor. I know that there were times that the body did its own thing and nobody could explain, but what was the point of becoming a doctor if you couldn't cure the illness?

We rode in silence for a while. Rochelle hummed along with the music on the radio. I continued to look out the window and watch the scenery pass me by. I felt as if my life was slowly spiraling out of my control. First, Dee sleeping with Sheba and now my mother. I couldn't even begin to imagine what would be the next hurdle in my life. I wanted to know what I had done to piss God off. Was I being punished? It didn't make sense to me.

"Do you think God is mad at me?" I wondered aloud.

"What?"

I turned my head to look at Rochelle while she drove. She kept her eyes on the road but I could tell that my question caught her off guard.

"Like, do you think because I continued to have sex with Dee that everything that's happening in my life is a punishment from God?"

"Sis, now you know that God doesn't operate that way. Sure, He chastises those He loves, but it's not punishment, per se."

"Hmm. It sure feels that way."

"It's a season you're going through. This season will pass before you know it. I know it seems crazy but you will make it through. I mean we all go through-"

"I used to date Rashad," I stated flatly, cutting her off.

The car started to slow down. Rochelle's face remained focused on the road but she briefly looked at me as she began to change lanes.

"What are you doing?"

She didn't respond. Instead she exited the interstate and pulled into a parking stall at the Quiktrip. She put the car in park, but left it running. She took off her seatbelt and turned to completely face me.

"Rashad who?" She asked quizzically.

I couldn't make eye contact with her. I focused my attention on my hands before responding, "Natalie's Rashad."

"Wow, Brooke. You're just now telling me this?"

I looked back up to see her hazel eyes piercing my way. If her look could kill, I died a thousand deaths in her car. I kept my eyes on her in hopes that she would read the sorrow in them. That she would soften enough for me to explain everything to her.

After what felt like an entirety she sighed and shook her head. "So, are you going to tell me the story or what?"

"I've known Rashad my whole life. We grew up together. He is my first everything. We dated all of high school up until our second year of college. He wanted to explore life in Athens so to speak. He hurt me in a way that I would've never expected. I just knew he was going to be the man I married and had beautiful chocolate babies with. By the time you and I met on line, we were through and I had erased him from my life. When Bree started to date Parker, I made it very clear I didn't want to know a thing about Rashad. I didn't know he was attending Emory until the Greek Picnic and that was the first time I had seen him since our break up. Recently, he reached out to me and we've been communicating.

Everything is cordial between us. We don't travel down memory lane or anything like that. I don't ask about Natalie and he never asks about Dee. We just check in with each other. I wanted to tell you the day I saw him at the picnic, but there wasn't a good time and there hasn't been a good time since."

Rochelle sat there silently taking in all that I told her. She then leaned over and hugged me. At first I was startled by her response, but then I embraced her back. My face became wet from my tears. It felt good to finally tell someone that I had reconnected with him. It was like a weight was lifted off my shoulders.

She sat back in her seat and playfully slapped my arm.

"Dammit, Brooke," she said, wiping tears from her eyes. "I don't know why you didn't tell me this before. What did you think I was going to do? Tell Natalie?"

I looked at her incredulously. "Well, yeah. That is your cousin. I know we're best friends, but you two are family."

She busted out laughing. Her tears continued to flow as she laughed harder. I smiled out of nervousness because I was concerned my best friend was bat shit crazy. Once she composed herself, she put her seatbelt back on and began driving towards the airport.

"Girl, let me get you to this airport so you don't miss your flight."

"Umm… okay."

Still chuckling she said, "If only you knew."

"Knew what?"

"Natalie and I are related by blood but that is as close as it gets between us."

"I'm not following you at all. You guys seem so close."

"No, what you see is her being close to me. Growing up there was talk that she was a little off. After her father died she was a whole new person. She would be super happy one minute and then she was whipping some random girl's tail for saying she had a big head. I mean petty stuff."

I didn't say anything. Shoot, what could I say? I was getting some piping hot tea and I was trying not to scald my mouth. She continued to explain that as kids, she remembered Natalie having to see a "special" doctor every week. Natalie's mom often came over to Rochelle's house for the girls to have play dates and to have private talks with her parents.

"At one point we were really close. I mean we were raised like sisters. But when I got back from TSU she had changed for the worse. To this day I don't know what happened, but something happened while she was attending TCU. The guy she was dating broke up with her and starting seeing someone else. The next thing I heard there was a restraining order taken out against her."

"What the world? Who took the order out?"

"Girl, the guy she was dating! Again, I don't know all the details. She wouldn't share with me and her mom was tight lipped as well. But something bad happened. I know that much. So you need to be careful. I know you and Rashad aren't doing anything. At least I hope not," she said, chuckling. "But bad things happen to people who my cousin feels have crossed her."

"Chile, I'm trying to fix my life. I got this baby and school to worry about. Rashad is the last person I'm worried about."

"Brooke, it's me you are talking to. I know you still love him. I remember that day we were leaving the club and you were telling me about the guy you dated. Do you remember that?"

"Vaguely."

"Well, I do. Matter of fact that would have been great time to tell me that it was Rashad. Anyway, if you've been holding onto that hurt for that long, there's something still there that hasn't been resolved. You need to handle that sooner than later."

I rolled my eyes and covered my ears. I heard Rochelle laugh and I laughed as well. I heard what she was saying, but I wasn't quite fully ready to admit that I still had feelings for him. As she pulled up to the airport terminals, I began to gather my belongings I had in the seat with me. Once the car stopped I got out and head to the backseat to grab my duffle bag. I poked my head back in the car to say goodbye.

"You make me sick, but I love you," I said, smiling at Rochelle.

"I know you do," she laughed. "Just be careful Brooke. Call me when you get in and send my love to the family. Love you girl."

Because of our little detour, I was rushing to get to my gate. The security checkpoint in Atlanta is known to be brutal. Thankfully, the line this morning wasn't as bad and I was able to get to my gate with ample time before the boarding process began.

Once at my gate, I pulled out the latest book by Kimberla Roby Lawson. She was one of my favorite authors. As I was starting to get in engrossed my book, the flight representative came over the P.A. system to inform us that we would be boarding within the next 15 minutes. That's when I saw him walking towards the trashcan not too far from where I was sitting. He was wearing blue jeans with a crisp white polo shirt. He was overdressed compared to me. I was in the stage of pregnancy were comfort took priority. That meant today I was rocking my Active Ego warm up gear.

"Rashad?" I called out as discreetly as I could before placing my book down across my lap. I didn't want to appear ghetto and holler out his name.

He turned in my direction and smiled at me. I returned his smile. Without thinking I moved my bag from the seat next to me, and gave him a silent invitation to come sit next to me. As soon as he settled in the seat next to me, there was a brief awkward silence between us.

"What are the chances that we would be heading back to Dallas on the same day and same time?" I said smiling at him.

He smiled as he said, "Kismet."

I nodded my head thoughtfully, "Kismet." I repeated softly.

Another awkward silence washed over us. It was weird sitting this close to him. The last time we were this close was at the Greek picnic. I felt as if an imaginary boundary had been breached and that this wasn't going to be last close encounter we would have. I continued to sit in silence and think, until he jolted me out of my head.

"So what happened to your accessory piece?"

What was he talking about? I thought to myself. I must have made a face at him, and he moved his gaze down to my left hand. I realized he was asking about my engagement ring. I quickly put my right hand on top of my left hand so he would no longer see my hands.

"It is a long story. One I'm sure that you don't want to hear right now."

"How long are you going to be home for?"

Again his question threw me off. "Just until Monday. I have to get back for my rotation and I still have lecture hall. Why?"

"Because I wanted to make sure we had time to talk."

We fell silent again and stayed that way until the airline representative started announcing the boarding process. We both stood up when Sky passengers were called to board the flight. As fate would have it we ended up sitting next to each the other.

"This is freaking crazy," I said as he sat down next to me after placing our bags in the overhead compartment.

"That's probably the understatement of the year." He laughed.

"Well, don't try to chat me up the whole flight. Nothing has changed. I still don't like flying."

"Brooke, you can't still be scared to fly? I'm on the plane with you this time. You can hold my hand if you get scared."

"Mmmhmm. I bet I can. If this plane goes down, you cannot save me. We're both going to die."

"Well, we're going to die one day. So why not together on a plane?"

I playfully punched his arm. "Shut up boy!" I laughed. "I need to pray and read my Bible before we take off and then I am going to sleep. We can talk once we land or something."

We ended up talking the entire flight. I can't remember what we talked about, but we laughed and had a great time. It reminded me of when we were younger and still just friends. I had forgotten how funny he could be.

When we got off the plane, he walked with me to ground transportation. We soon discovered that Parker was picking us both up from the airport.

"You realize this was all a setup by our siblings?" I told him as we waited for Parker.

"I know that now," he said, shaking his head in disbelief. "I wasn't even paying attention when he said that he thought we got in on the same day."

"Bree told me to fly in on this day. I'm going to kick her butt when I see her."

We both laughed and continued to have small talk until Parker picked us up. I didn't know what to expect from this weekend, but I could tell that it was going to be an interesting one to say the very least.

Chapter 19

Natalie

I had to make sure I was reading his text correctly.

I'm going home this weekend. So you will have to come get your stuff when I get back.

I wonder why Rashad was going home. He never went home during the middle of the semester. There must be an emergency going on with his family. Why wouldn't he tell me? I know we aren't together, but us not being together is temporary. He's just upset because of how I popped up on him that day in the café with Denise. However, I've still been at every event that was important to him to show my loyalty. I mean, we're friends and he knows that I love him. I need to find out how I can get home this weekend and then I can prove to him that I'm here for him.

I sat down at my desk in my spare bedroom and thought about how I could get home on short notice. Money wasn't an issue but where I was going to stay was. I know that I couldn't expect to stay at Rashad's house. I sighed as I picked up the phone to make a call to the one person that irritated me the most.

"Hey sweet girl," the voice answered upon picking up the phone. I rolled my eyes in disgust but made sure my tone didn't reflect how I felt on the inside.

"Hi, Mommy."

"I'm surprised to hear from you during the day. Well, actually I'm surprised to hear from you at all. I usually call you. You must want something."

She laughed at her last statement. I wanted to slap her. She always thought her jokes were funny but they weren't. I forced myself to laugh along with her, because I did want something.

"Mommy, why do you always assume I want something? I call you all the time."

"Mmmhmm."

"I think I want to come home this weekend and spend some time with you."

She didn't say anything for a minute. I imagined her sorting papers around on her desk as she tried to think of a way to gently respond to me.

"Nat, are you okay? Everything alright with you and Rashad? I know you're doing well with your classes."

"Yes, Mama everything is fine. I just need to get away. That's all. I'm sure you can understand that and I'm sure Dr. Bellman would be fine with it."

"Well, how long are you going to be here for? Just the weekend I assume?"

"Yes ma'am."

She got quiet again. She was really pissing me off acting like she didn't want me to come home. I didn't need her permission to do anything.

"You know you don't have to seek permission to stay here. You know that right? But I think you should stay until Monday and see Dr. Bellman before you leave. If she's not available then I would suggest seeing Dr. Hall. Just to check in."

"Fine Mom. I gotta go and see if I can use my frequent flyer miles. I'll email my flight info."

"Okay baby. I love you, Natalie."

I disconnected the phone call. I hope that I didn't have to fight my mama this weekend. Again.

Chapter 20

Brooke

I waved goodbye as the guys dropped me off at my parents' house. Rashad had been so kind to bring my stuff in the house for me. There was a brief moment of awkwardness as he prepared to walk back to the car. We both were trying to process how to say goodbye to one another. Finally, he leaned down to hug me. We embraced a little longer than we should have. When we finally separated, I diverted my eyes to avoid looking at him and stood behind the open front door until he made it back to the car.

Once I got settled in, I called my dad at his job to let him know I made it home. He sounded exhausted but said we all were going to hospital in a few hours to visit with my mother. I figured I would use that time to get some rest. I was still dealing pregnancy fatigue despite being close to my second trimester. Being fatigued made things challenging but I rather be fatigued then deal with morning sickness.

I must have fell asleep with my phone in my hand because when it vibrated in my hand it startled the mess out of me. Without looking at the caller ID, I answered the phone.

"Hello," I said groggily. I started to close my eyes again until I heard his voice.

"What's up with you? You sleep?" he asked.

"Who is this?"

"You wrote me off that quickly, babe?"

I was fully alert now. I couldn't believe that he had the audacity to call me.

"What do you want, Donovan?" I asked with a chill in my voice.

"I was calling to see how you and the baby are doing."

"We're doing fine," I answered flatly.

He became quiet. I had no intentions of holding a conversation with him. If it wasn't for the fact that I was carrying his child I would have nothing to do with him.

I heard him clear his throat before saying, "I'm sorry, Brooke. This isn't how I wanted things to be between us."

I still said nothing.

"Are you still there?"

I sighed. "Donovan, I'm out of town right now taking care of family business. I honestly don't have time to entertain this conversation with you. I can't."

"Is everything okay with your family?" he asked, sounding genuinely concerned.

"Things will be fine. Look, I gotta go."

"Brooke, can I come see you when you get back home?"

I rolled my eyes and took a deep breath. I started to respond but instead disconnected the call. I still had at least 30 minutes of sleep to get in before it was time for me to go see my mother.

I never liked the way hospitals smelled or felt. They were always cold and smelled of sick people. Yet, I was on track to becoming a doctor and would spend the majority of my time in the hospital. Irony at its finest.

My father, sisters, and I arrived at the hospital in time to speak with my mom's doctor. Doctor Lawson was a tall, lanky and balding brother. He was doing his best to hold onto what little hair he had left on his head but it was losing battle. Despite his balding, he was an attractive man with a calm demeanor.

He was speaking with another doctor who appeared to be a few years my senior. He put me in the mind of a young Matthew McConaughey. He was fine! My mother was being poked and prodded by the nurses in her room and hadn't noticed us when we walked in.

"Hi Mommy," I spoke as we entered in the room.

Everyone stopped talking and looked our way. My mother smiled and waved at us. She looked tired but was still alert. The doctors and nurses greeted us warmly. They moved out the way to allow us to fully enter and give us some space to get settled in the available seats. Once the nurses finished gathering the information they needed, they left the room. I walked over to my mother and gave her a kiss on the forehead.

"How are you feeling, Mama?" I asked softly.

"I'm doing well. Considering how I felt before now, I'm well, baby."

My father and sisters walked over and greeted my mother as well. The doctors, who had remained in the room, were waiting patiently near the door. I assumed they wanted to stay around and answer any questions.

"Doctors, this is my daughter who is studying medicine in Atlanta," my mother said, grabbing my arm. She said it with so much pride in her voice. I smiled at the doctors and shook their hands.

"It's a pleasure to meet you, Brooke." the Matthew McConaughey lookalike said.

"Good Lord. He even has a southern drawl, too," I thought to myself.

"Likewise," I said with a smile.

"Yes, your mother has told me so much about you. We wanted to wait to meet you and answer any questions you may have. We both were once young medical students. Well, I've been out of school a lot longer than Dr. Davidson," Dr. Lawson said.

"Well, I'm not here to step on any toes, but I would be lying if I said I didn't research my mother's symptoms. The good thing is that I don't have to rely on the Mayo clinic or WebMD."

We all laughed.

"That's a great thing. We would actually love to hear what you have to say. This could be some great experience for you. We know you're studying to become an OB/GYN, but your mother told us that you're super smart. Like most doctors," Dr. Davidson said with a wink.

I felt my mocha skin get warm as I put my head down to avoid making any further eye contact with him. He was definitely flirting with me and I wasn't sure how to act.

"So do any of you doctors have an idea of what is going on with my wife?" my father said with a hint of annoyance in his voice. He brought all of us back to reality. I had totally forgot that him and my sisters were in the room. I was so caught with Dr. Davidson's looks that I was in another world.

"Ahh, yes sir," Dr. Lawson spoke. "However, we would like for Brooke to tell us what she has researched."

"With all due respect. My daughter ain't no doctor yet and I would rather her experiment with another patient that isn't her mother," my father responded matter of factly.

"Oh, Gerald hush," my mother said. "I requested this. I want Brooke to do this. The doctors have already explained what's going on. They were doing that before you all got here. Calm down, honey."

My father sighed deeply and rolled his eyes, but he didn't say anything else. All of sudden I felt pressure to be correct. If for no other reason to not hear my father's mouth later.

"Well…" I said slowly looking around the room. Both of my sisters smiled at me while my dad frowned. "Once I was able to talk to my sister and get an idea of what happened with my mother on the day she passed out, she shared with me that my mother had been complaining of a rapid heartbeat, confusion, and was sweating more than usual. At first I thought it was just stress. She is superintendent and all. But then I thought a little harder and did some research on low blood sugar. Based upon her symptoms, I think she has insulinoma; especially with her passing out."

There was a brief moment of silence in the room. I looked over at my mom who was smirking at me. I looked back at the doctors waiting for them to validate my diagnosis.

"Very good Doctor," Dr. Lawson spoke. He sounded like a proud dad. Dr. Davidson smiled at me and nodded his head.

"Well, what does that mean?" my father piped up from behind me.

"Basically, your wife's body is overproducing insulin and has caused a tumor to form on her pancreas. In most cases, the tumor is benign and surgery treats the issue. We aren't sure what could have caused this to happen to her and it is very possible that she has had this going on for awhile before it came to head last week. We are looking to do surgery on Monday morning. We have completed all the testing that makes us confident in our diagnosis."

"So Mommy is going to be alright?" my baby sister asked.

"She will be fine. We are confident this is noncancerous and that she will come through surgery well based upon her current health status. Of course there are always risks with surgery and post surgery but we will monitor her and take care of her."

"Well, this has to be the best news I've gotten all week!" I exclaimed. I hugged my mother and gave her a kiss on the forehead.

My daddy playfully pushed me out the way to give my mother a kiss on the lips. She smiled lovingly at my father.

He held her hand and wiped an escaped tear from his eyes with his free hand.

My sisters and I all hugged each other. There were tears of joy among all of us. The doctors gave us some more information before saying goodbye. It felt great to genuinely smile again.

Chapter 21

Rashad

After Parker and I dropped Brooke off at home we stopped by In-N-Out Burger to get something to eat. I made it a point to stop here to eat every time I came for a visit. I remember when they first started popping up in the Dallas area, everybody and their mama was in line to get a burger. We decided to eat inside the restaurant before heading back to the house.

"So, I'm preaching my first sermon tonight at this youth revival. You gonna come through and support your baby brother?" Parker asked in between bites of his burger.

I took a sip of my soda before responding. My brother knew that I didn't do church. The only times I went to church at home was if my mother begged me to go. My father ruined church for me a long time ago and I found it hard to believe in a God that would allow my father to preach.

"I can't man. I was going to try and get up with some of the guys," I said, trying to sound convincing. I knew damn well I was going to sit at my parents' house and do nothing.

"Come on, Shad. This is my first sermon. I'm not going to have anyone there. Bree is probably not going to come because of everything going on with her mom. I didn't tell

Mom or Dad about it because of what is going on in the house. I really could use some support. Plus it's a youth revival. I'm only going to be speaking for about 15-20 minutes tops."

I gave my brother the 'yeah right' look at his latter statement. He and I both knew that was the number one lie pastors told in the pulpit. My dad was notorious for saying that he had only five minutes left in his sermon. That dude would be up there for an additional 20 minutes. It would be that one church mother that would encourage him to take his time and that's what he would do. There were plenty of times I thought about walking his seat up to him so that he would be encouraged to wrap his sermon up.

Parker laughed before responding, "I'm serious. They have two other pastors speaking tonight as well. This church is pretty strict about the timing. You know you ain't about to do nothing for real but sit at home and think about Brooke."

"Whatever man," I said, trying to brush off what he said about Brooke.

"You know it's true, bro."

I shook my head and ignored him. "Anyway," I said. "I will come to hear you preach. Just don't be up there all day and don't be trying to have me stay there all day either."

Parker smiled and said, "I won't, Shad. I think that you'll have a great time."

I shook my head and kept eating my food. We sat in the restaurant a little while longer talking about nothing. I was proud of the man my little brother was becoming. I could tell that he was passionate about preaching and that it was something he really enjoyed doing. One thing I admired about him was his ability to see the good in everything and everybody. There was not a person he couldn't get along with. At least not to my knowledge. That's probably why he was able to handle my father as well as he did. I guess I could learn a thing or two from him.

The youth choir was rocking! I tried my hardest not to clap along to the music, but my foot got to tapping and the next thing I knew I was standing up clapping my hands to the song.

The youth revival at Friendship Church of God in Christ was packed with young and old folks. I, of course, got there early, but right before the choir sang it was announced that they had opened up the overflow room to help accommodate the folks who were still waiting in the lobby. I was amazed to see the amount of young folks praising God. It was unlike anything I've ever witnessed. Sure, I had grown up going to similar functions but I was usually outside of the revival with my guys getting high or playing craps.

My brother told me that the other pastors preaching were known nationally and that it was a pretty big deal for him to be put on the program with them. He was nervous as hell, too. Parker was scheduled last to speak. Now, I had heard of these pastors before and they were a big deal, but I was confident that my brother would be able to pull it off.

"Amen," Parker said as he reached the podium after the choir sang their last song. "Give it up for the choir. Y'all did your thing. If you can't feel the presence of God in this room, you need to check your pulse because He is in the building tonight," he said to a resounding hand clap from the church.

"Before I begin I want to open up with prayer. If everyone would please bow your heads and close your eyes."

After he finished praying he began his sermon. I remember chuckling at the sermon title, "God, do your care or nah?" I listened and watched my baby brother speak with an authority and passion that I never heard before. Not even our father sounded this passionate when he gave his Sunday morning sermons. Not only did he have my attention, but he had the attention of everyone in attendance as well. Again, I found myself fully engaged in the service.

"I know many of you have experienced hardships in your life. You wonder if God saw that time that family member touched you in a way that they weren't supposed to. You wonder if He saw that time you were belittled by your parents for not living up to an unrealistic expectation. Or even that time you were struggling in school. But I want you to know that He has seen and heard you. He has not forgotten about you and if you hold on, you will reap the harvest. Don't worry about who has hurt you in your past. Keep your eyes on the powerful God and watch Him work things out in your favor. For what the enemy meant for evil, God will turn that thing around for your good and His glory!"

The church erupted with shouts of amens and hallelujahs. The organist began to play and one of the mothers began to shout. In the midst of her shouting, she lost her wig. The ushers quickly stood around her in a feeble attempt to hide her silver cornrows. There were young people shouting and praising God. I looked up on stage to see my brother doing a little two step in Jesus' name.

Once people began to settle down, the organist slowed the tempo down and my brother invited people to the altar to receive salvation. I felt compelled to go to the altar but I couldn't seem to move my feet. I stood there frozen. I watched as dozens of young people made their way to the altar. I wiped something wet from my face. It was a tear that had escaped. I quickly put my head down for the remaining part of altar call.

Chapter 22

Rashad

I sat downstairs the next morning eating a bowl of cereal. I had the television on the sports channel but I kept it muted. My mind was still on last night. It had been a while since I felt moved or, as the church folk say, convicted. It was as if God himself was trying to talk to me. I wanted to talk to Parker about it but on the ride home he got a call from Bree and they spoke the entire ride. Since I wasn't able to talk to him about it, I took it as a sign that may be it was a fluke and that I was just excited about my baby brother doing what he loved.

My mother walked in the kitchen, throwing her keys down on the counter as she entered. I must have startled her because she jumped when saw me. I looked at my mother puzzled but kept eating my cereal.

She's up early for a Saturday morning, I thought to myself before telling her good morning.

"Good morning, son. Did you and Parker have a good time hanging out last night?" she asked as she made herself a cup of tea and sat down at the table with me.

"Yeah. We had a good time."

"That's good. Your dad should be back home from his conference tomorrow and I'm thinking of calling the caterer to do dinner."

Her tone was flat and she had a distant look in her eyes. I could tell something was heavy on her mind and it looked as if she been crying.

"Mom, what's wrong?" I asked, tentatively.

Instead of responding, she pulled a large envelope out of her purse. She placed the envelope down in front of me. I looked at it but didn't move to pick it up. I waited patiently for her to tell me what was going on.

She took a sip of her tea and closed her eyes. It was as if she was praying. Our eyes met when she opened them a few seconds later. I looked down at my empty bowl to avoid making things awkward. She took a deep breath before speaking.

"Your father is having affairs," she stated matter of factly.

"You mean an affair?" I asked.

She looked me directly in the eyes and said, "No, son. I mean affairs. Plural. Two that I've been made aware of today."

"Today? Mom, what are you talking about?"

"I received an email earlier this week from a young lady who attends one of our sister churches, Faith COGIC. She informed me that she had been seeing your father for the past year. Initially, I blew off the email and deleted it. When I didn't respond, she sent a follow up email and included pictures of the two of them together. She also sent additional pictures with her email."

She paused briefly to take another sip of her tea. She picked up the envelope she had laid on the table and removed the contents. There was an email and several pictures. I grabbed the pictures and began to inspect each one of them. I then proceeded to read the emails between the young lady and my mother. I was left speechless. Literally, there was not a word, phrase, or thought that I could formulate.

"So, of course I had to meet Tasha because I wanted to hear from her mouth how on earth she got involved with your father. I clearly got more than what I bargained for in my talk with her this morning. Apparently, your father has been dealing with her since she was 17 and a senior in high school. However, they didn't have sex until she turned 18. He would take her as far as Austin or even Houston to spend time with her. She said he told her that he was unhappy in his marriage and that he loved her. You know the usual stuff men say when they are cheating on their wives. She realized he didn't love her when he gave her money to get an abortion."

"An abortion?" I asked incredulously.

My mother ignored my question and continued, "She got the abortion only to discover he was sleeping with Minister Miller's wife. You remember Minister Miller over the youth department? Apparently, Tasha saw your dad and Simone kissing outside of hotel during a youth convocation. She even said I was there, but I don't remember that. Anyway, Tasha began following them around and discovered that he had gotten Simone pregnant as well. You can see that from the picture with him rubbing on her belly. She just started showing, too. Here I am planning her baby shower and this woman is pregnant with my husband's bastard child."

By now my mother was crying. Not hysterically, but tears were flowing like a river down her face as she spoke each angry word. I reread the last email from Tasha.

Mrs. Wallace, I'm sorry to bring this type of news to you. I realize now that I was wrong for what I did and I wish I could take it all back. I never thought in a million years that I would ever sleep with a married man, get pregnant and abort my first child for the man that said he loved me. Initially, my reason for telling you about our affair was to hurt him. I really thought he would be with me. But when you spoke at our young adult conference last month, I knew that you had a right to know about the kind of man your husband really is. I hope you still want to meet with me so I can tell you everything in person. Again, I'm so very sorry for any pain this is causing you.

I shook my head. It was a good thing my father wasn't coming home tonight, because there is no telling what I would do to him. I hated that man. My mother is a God fearing, classy woman who has been an excellent wife and mother. This is how he chooses to repay her?

I got up out of my chair and walked over to my mother. I leaned down to give her a hug. She cried deeply onto me. When I stood back my t-shirt was soaked from her tears. She grabbed a napkin to blow her nose and wipe at her eyes.

"I'm sorry to have to bring this to you. I know that you have your own life going, but I wanted to be honest with you," she said in between tears.

"Don't apologize, Mama. You tell me what you want to do and how you want to handle this situation. Have you told Parker yet?"

"Two things I know for sure. I'm going to inform the elder board this coming week and I'll start the divorce proceedings on Monday. Other than that I have no clue what I'm doing and no I haven't told Parker. I was waiting until you got into town to tell you both but I saw you first. I will tell him. I think right now I am going to lay down. I need to be alone for a while."

With that she went upstairs to her room. I sat back down at the kitchen table and looked over everything again.

"Dude, are you listening to me?" an agitated Parker asked.

"Huh?" I said, lost.

Disappointed with my response, Parker shook his head as he took a bite of his nachos. We were downstairs in the basement of my parents' house watching college football. Parker was talking a mile a minute about something, but I was still thinking about the things our mother shared with me earlier that day. I wasn't even sure I wanted to go to church tomorrow to see our dad or the woman he got pregnant.

"I said the girls wanted to know if we're going to stop by the hospital to see about Mama Jones. Bree also wanted to invite us over for Sunday dinner. Do you want to go?"

"Oh, that's cool bruh."

"Dang what is going on with you? You been acting all weird since I got home from the gym this morning."

I hesitated for a second on if I should tell Parker what was going with our parents. Our mom hadn't come back downstairs since she and I talked. If she wanted something she would text me to bring it her, but other than that she wasn't in the mood. But how could I not tell my brother what was going on? He needed to know, in the event something popped off at church.

"Yo, you are not going to believe what Mom told me today."

Chapter 23

Natalie

Nothing about this trip home was going according to my plan. First, my flight out of Atlanta got cancelled on Friday morning and I ended up on a later one. I didn't arrive in Dallas until early Saturday morning. Of course my mother had arranged for me to see my counselor at o'dark thirty on Saturday. I don't even know how she got me a Saturday appointment but here I sat talking about nothing in this counseling session.

"So Natalie, is there anything else you want to talk about? How are you and Rashad doing? How's school?" Dr. Bellman asked.

I rolled my eyes. I didn't want to be here. For one, my black ass could be sleep right now, and two, I needed to figure out where Rashad was. I had been trying to figure out how I could accidentally bump into him while here, but from the looks of things this was going to be a busted trip.

"I'm sorry, Natalie. Do you not want to be here?" her voice showing a hint of an attitude.

I shook my head. "But it's no offense to you. I just planned for my weekend to be a little different. I wasn't planning on seeing you until Monday."

"I understand. Well we're here now and we have an hour to talk. So, what do you want to talk about?" her tone softening again.

I could tell that she wasn't going to let up. I couldn't blame her for wanting to do her job. I didn't want to disappoint either, so I put forth my best acting skills to move our session forward. Maybe if I got of here in enough time, I can make an impromptu visit by Rashad's neighborhood.

Chapter 24

Rashad

Sunday couldn't have arrived soon enough. After Parker and I had talked about the things going on with our parents, we cancelled hanging out with Brooke and Bree Saturday night. Parker and I had planned on confronting Minister Simone after church. We were going to confront my father once we all got home. However, my mother had different plans that even Stevie Wonder couldn't see coming.

"Shad! Parker, wait a minute!" my mother called after us once service was over. We stopped in our tracks and turned to acknowledge her. We were getting ready to walk down the stairs to where the youth church was held. A few church members had stopped her before she could make her way to us. A few moments later she stood before us flashing that beautiful smile. She looked refreshed and not distraught over her cheating husband.

"Hey Mom," Parker said giving her a kiss on the cheek. I followed suit.

"So, I need you guys to come with me to the hospital. I promised Mrs. Jones that I would bring you, Rashad, to come see her before you left town tomorrow. She's having her surgery in the morning. Are you guys ready now?"

Parker and I exchanged quick glances before telling her that we could leave now. My mother wanted us to ride together and leave Parker's car at the church. We arrived at the hospital in time to see Brooke's family visiting as well. Mrs. Jones was finishing up a conversation with a nurse. Mr. Jones was sitting in the recliner watching football, while Brooke and her sisters were talking and eating at the table in the room.

"Hey Viv!" Mrs. Jones said as my mother walked over to give her a hug.

"Hey Renae!" my mother said.

"Shad, it's been awhile since I've seen you, honey. How's school going?" Mrs. Jones asked.

I walked over to give her a hug and spoke, "I know. School is fine. Just ready to graduate."

"I know you are. Parker, you going to eat all of Bree's food and not come say nothing to me?" she scolded playfully at him.

We all laughed as Parker walked over to give Mrs. Jones a hug. There wasn't enough seats for everyone to sit, but Mr. Jones and Brooke's youngest sister decided to head home to get some rest. Mr. Jones was coming back to the hospital later to stay the night. I went and sat next to Brooke while my mother and her mother caught up. I tried to take one of Brooke's wings but she popped my hand.

"Boy, don't make me hurt you," she laughed before offering me a wing.

"So, what did you two end up doing last night?" Bree asked suspiciously to both Parker and I.

"Would you believe me if I told you that we sat around and watched football?" Parker asked.

Bree smirked. "Of course, I would. That's all you ever want to do on a Saturday night."

We all laughed. I saw Bree wipe something off Parker's face as he was eating some of her food. I admired them for a moment. These two were in their own world and not focused on anyone else but each other.

Parker and Bree had been dating for about a year or so now. Although we grew up together, those two were in different circles. To be honest, I think Bree was into thug types. Parker was far from anybody's thug. I don't even know if my brother can fight because I would always fight whoever thought they wanted to fight him.

"Don't stare so hard." Brooke's voice came out of nowhere.

"Huh?" I said as I turned to look her. She was smiling at me with that million dollar smile.

"Huh nothing. A penny for your thoughts?" she asked.

I shook my head. "Its nothing."

"If you say so. How are you and Natalie doing?"

"We not."

I heard Bree start coughing. I turned to see her take a sip of her drink, while Parker tried to stifle a laugh. I looked back at Brooke who was shaking her head at her sister.

"You alright girl?" Brooke asked as if she was annoyed.

"Yeah girl. So when did y'all break up?" Bree asked, ignoring her sister's annoyance.

"I mean it's been at least a month or so since we broke up. I been trying to get her to come get her stuff from my place, but it's like she is stalling."

"That's because that crazy girl thinks you two are still together," Brooke said, laughing. Bree chuckled as well but I didn't see anything funny.

"Well, she may be crazy, but she ain't that crazy to think that," I said as convincingly as I could muster. I didn't quite believe that and apparently neither did anyone sitting at that table.

"Oh okay." Was all Brooke said.

There were a few moments of silence at our table. The only sounds in the room were the voices of our mothers talking a mile a minute and the medical equipment Brooke's mother was hooked up to.

"So, what happened with you and old boy?" I asked Brooke. My question took her off guard. Her eyes grew with surprise but quickly went back to their normal size. This time her sister did not cough, instead whispered something to Parker. They both rose from the table and said they were going walk down to the vending machine.

I looked back at Brooke who was now looking out of the hospital window. It was obvious she was deep in thought. I waited patiently for her to speak again.

"We aren't together," she said finally. Her voice barely above a whisper.

"I'm sor-" I started to say.

She raised her hand to cut me off. "There's nothing for you to be sorry about. Our relationship was on life support for a little while now but things took a turn for the worse before I found out about my mother."

"Are you going to be okay?"

"I don't have a choice but to be. It's no longer about me anymore."

I wasn't sure what that last statement meant, but before I could ask her to clarify, my mother announced that it was time for us to be heading back home. She had received a text that the caterer had completed dinner, and was preparing to leave our house. Parker and Bree still hadn't made it back to the room.

"Brooke, do you and your sister want to come over for dinner? I'm sure you girls will be hungry again," my mother asked.

"Oh, sure Mrs. Wallace. Mama, are you going to be okay with us leaving?" Brooke asked as she walked over to mother's bedside.

"That's fine. I'm tired anyway. I need to get some rest before your father heads back. Brittany is going to be spending the night at Justine's house so she can get to school in the morning. So don't worry about rushing home or anything."

Brooke leaned down and gave her mother a hug and kiss. I came behind her and did the same.

"Alright, Viv. You get some rest. I will come by tomorrow to check on you and see how everything went. I love you, sis."

"I love you, too. Oh and don't forget to tell me how everything goes."

"Trust me, I won't."

They laughed and hugged each other. As we walked out of Mrs. Jones' hospital room, we ran into Bree and Parker. Bree and Brooke walked alongside my mother to the parking lot. I quietly and quickly filled Parker in about the new dinner plans.

"I guess we'll have to wait to confront Dad," Parker said.

I nodded my head in agreement but didn't realize that the confrontation would still take place. It just wouldn't go down as we planned.

Chapter 25

Rashad

As soon as we walked in the house, we were greeted by smells of honey glazed turkey, collard greens, black eye peas, candied yams, macaroni and cheese, cornbread, rolls, and red velvet cake. It was not unusual to have our Sunday dinners catered, but there was usually enough to feed four to six people. This time it looked as if we were going to be feeding at least 20.

"Dang Mama. Who are you trying to feed? The whole congregation stopping through?" Parker asked, jokingly.

My mother smiled as she inspected the dinner table. She then placed sealed manila envelopes under each of the dinner plates.

"We have guests coming over and I wanted to make sure that we had enough for everyone to eat. Brooke and Bree can you go grab some extra napkins from the kitchen please? They're sitting on the counter next to the refrigerator."

Just then, the alarm system chirped to inform us that someone walked in the house. I heard the girls speak to my father. Both my brother and I quickly followed my mother into the kitchen. My mother walked in the kitchen and warmly greeted my father. He leaned down to give her a quick peck on the lips. My mother then took his coat, briefcase, and hat and went upstairs to their room. Brooke and Bree had walked out of the kitchen to place the napkins on the table and to get ready for dinner. My father poured himself a drink and walked past my brother and I as if we were nonexistent. I could tell Parker was surprised that my father didn't acknowledge neither one of us.

"Asshole," I whispered as we followed him back in the dining room.

My father took his seat at the head of the table. I saw him reach for the manila envelope and inspect it curiously. Before he could open it, my mother walked into the dining room. She playfully popped his hand.

"No, no," she said wagging her index finger. "We'll open that later on."

Before he could protest, the doorbell rang. My mother smiled and clapped her hands as she headed to the front door.

"Do you all know who's here?" my father asked, looking at me.

"Nah," I said dryly and took my seat next to Brooke.

My mother's laughter was heard before she entered the dining room. She was followed by two of the church's most prominent elder board members, their wives, and the Millers. Something told me that this dinner wasn't going to be the usual Sunday dinner. Elder Henry Williams and Elder Jonathan Scott had the power to make things happen not only in our church, but in the sister churches around the metro area. Not only did they have power but they had action and money to back it.

My mother directed everyone to their seat. I was just as surprised as Simone Miller, when my mother insisted that she have the seat next to my father's head chair. I didn't pay attention to the empty seat that was on the opposite side of my father and in front of Simone.

We said grace and made our plates. About 15 minutes into our meal, the doorbell rang again.

"Please excuse me," my mother said as she rose from the table to answer the door.

I thought my father was going to choke on his food when he saw Tasha walk in. He quickly recovered and continued eating. I heard my mother direct Tasha where to sit after she made her plate. Tasha looked uncomfortable as she took her seat next to my father. I saw her look down to where my mother was sitting, who gave her a reassuring smile. The next few minutes changed my family dynamic in a way that I'm sure none of us could fathom.

"Michael, would you like to introduce Tasha to everyone?" my mother asked my father. Her voice was sweet but her eyes showed a fire behind them. My father didn't miss a beat.

"I would if I knew who this young lady was." He then turned to Tasha and asked, "Are you new to the area or something?"

Before Tasha could respond my mother let out a hearty laugh.

"Michael, Michael, Michael," my mother said in a sing song voice, while shaking her head disapprovingly. "I guess we'll have to do this differently. Everyone please open your envelopes. The contents are in a particular order and I'll direct you as such. Brooke and Bree, I hadn't planned on having you ladies over but feel free to follow along with the boys."

Everyone, except my father, tore into their envelopes. My father kept eating but kept his gaze on my mother. At first everyone was silent as we all looked at the pictures of my dad and Simone. There were pictures of them holding hands, kissing, and even one of him rubbing her protruding belly.

"What in the world are these Bishop Wallace?" Elder Scott asked my father accusingly.

By now nobody was eating their food, but we were all waiting for my father to respond to the elder's question. My father shrugged his shoulders, took a sip of his of drink, and continued to gaze at my mother. Simone was looking like a deer in headlights and began rocking back and forth in her chair. Her husband's face remained stoic and focused on my father.

"These are pictures of what appears to be you and Simone in a relationship," my mother answered for him. "Which is funny because the both of you are married." My mother cut her eyes over to Simone who refused to look my mother's way.

"Again, I ask you Michael. Would you care to introduce Tasha to everyone?"

My father remained silent but it was obvious he was becoming increasingly upset. Instead of responding, he picked up his envelope. His face remained calm as he reviewed each document in the packet. My mother didn't protest.

"How did you get any of this?" he asked calmly.

"Is that really your concern at this moment? How I got any of these documents?" My mother shook her head in disgust. "This is going to my final time asking you to introduce Tasha to everyone. If you won't introduce her, then I will gladly make the introduction."

"I ain't got to do a damn thing, woman," my father spat.

"Wrong answer," my mother said before continuing. "Simone, I want you to meet Tasha. Tasha was sleeping with my husband around the same time you were. In fact, my husband met this wonderful young lady when she was about 17, but had enough sense to wait to sleep with her until she was of age."

"Is this true Bishop?" Elder Williams asked in shocking disbelief.

My mother turned to the Elder and said, "Oh, it's true. Tasha is the one who took the pictures of Simone and my husband, after she aborted her baby. The baby that my husband fathered. If you look in your packages, you will see the receipt from the abortion clinic and text messages from my husband saying he was sorry for having her kill their baby."

There was an audible gasp from the women at the table. The men shook their heads in disbelief at my mother's latest revelation. Everyone began flipping through the documents to find what my mother was talking about.

Sure enough there was a receipt from the clinic and the screen shots of the text messages between my father and Tasha. If I thought my father was low down before, I knew without a shadow of doubt he was truly the scum of the earth. In one of the texts he told Tasha that they could try again for a baby after the divorce between my mother and him was final. All of this information was more than what my mother shared with me yesterday morning.

"But that's not even the best part of the story. Minister Jerome would you like to add something to the discussion."

Minister Jerome Miller, Simone's husband, had been sitting quietly the entire time. I noticed that his envelope was still under his dinner plate. Then it dawned on me that he and my mother were in cahoots together. Minister Jerome turned to his crying wife and spoke in an even, calm voice.

"As some of you know, Simone and I struggled for years with getting pregnant. It wasn't until recently that we decided to see a fertility specialist about what could be the issue. It was recommended that a semen analysis be performed to ensure that sperm was not an issue. It was determined that my sperm count was so low and that it would take a miracle for me to get Simone pregnant. There was talk of us having to use a donor sperm. So, Simone and I decided to pray about it but keep trying.

In the meantime, I went and got a second opinion from a urologist. This time the report said I had zero sperm count. The day I got my results back, is the same day that Simone told me she was pregnant. Due to the excitement of her being pregnant, I never shared with her the results from the second doctor, but something told me that the baby she is carrying wasn't my baby."

"But this is your baby, Jerome!" exclaimed Simone as she attempted to put a hand on his shoulder. Jerome jumped back so fast you would have thought he was having a seizure of some sort.

"Don't you dare touch me!" Jerome spat at Simone. He then turned his attention to my father. Seething, he said to my father, "You call yourself a man of God. You don't know how bad I want to kill you for messing up my family."

"Nigga ain't nobody mess up your family. It ain't my fault that you can't control your woman! Don't think I won't whip your ass for trying to disrespect me up in my house!" my father spat at Jerome.

The two men stared at each other. Both men's nostrils were flaring as one waited for the other to make a move. My father had at least 50 or so pounds over Jerome. Jerome, however, was a former pro basketball player and maintained his athletic build over the years. Plus Jerome had youth on his side and would be a lot quicker to move if my father did decide to strike first.

"Now Bishop I think we should all calm down," Elder Williams said, calmly.

"I agree," Elder Scott said.

My father looked at Tasha, who had backed away from the dining room table. She looked as if she was ready to take off running if she had to.

"And you!" my father said, pointing his finger angrily at her. "What the hell do you think you're doing? You trying to set me up? You know damn well I ain't make you get no abortion. You knew what it was when we got together."

By now my father was standing up and had started moving towards Tasha. My mother rose from the table and began to walk towards Tasha. As my mother moved closer to Tasha, my father turned his attention towards my mother. It was at this point I got up to get closer to my mother. I felt Brooke grab my hand, but I shook it off me.

"And you, stupid bitch!"

This stopped my mother in her tracks. I was behind her so I couldn't read her face, but I imagined she was in shock. But no more in shock than I was when I saw my father open hand slap my mother in the face. Hard. She fell to the ground grabbing her face. The last thing I heard was screaming as I threw the first punch, connecting with my father's jaw.

After that all I saw was red.

Chapter 26

Brooke

"Oh, my damn!" I kept repeating in my head as I tried to get my pregnant butt up to check on Rashad's mom. I was too stunned to move because Rashad and his dad were going for blows. There was blood going everywhere but I wasn't able to tell who was bleeding, let alone where they were bleeding from. The men that were present were trying to separate the two, but it was proving to be an impossible feat.

Finally, Parker and one of the elders were able to grab Rashad off of their dad. Mr. Jones was on the floor, breathing through his mouth, which was busted up pretty bad. I couldn't tell if Rashad's nose was broken or not.

I looked behind me and saw Mrs. Jones and Tasha huddled together in the living room. Both of the ladies were crying. I think all of the ladies were. The elder wives were hysterical as they ran to comfort Mrs. Jones and Tasha. Simone was still sitting in her chair, rocking back and forth, mumbling something under her breath as tears kept falling from her face. Bree, however, was staring at me. I could tell she was waiting for me to direct her to do something to assist. I quickly went into doctor mode.

"Bree, I need you to grab a few towels. Hand one towel to Rashad for his nose. Another towel needs to have a few ice cubes in it for Mr. Jones."

Bree nodded her head and took off to grab the items I requested. I took another survey of the room and tried to mentally assess my priorities. I'm not sure I was prepared for this with my limited medical training, but that was the nerves talking and I had to jump in. As I moved towards Simone, I could hear Parker trying to calm Rashad down.

"*Good luck!*" I thought. It had been a while since I'd seen Rashad this angry and getting him to calm to down was going to take Jesus coming down to earth.

Jesus was also going to have to come have a talk with His other child, Rashad's father. He was still cussing while holding the towel against his lip. The other elder was working on trying to calm him down. Jerome, Simone's husband, was tending to Rashad's mother.

"Hi, Simone," I said once I got to her. She was still mumbling and rocking back and forth.

"It's his baby," she mumbled. She hadn't acknowledged my presence.

I gently placed a hand on her shoulder. She stopped rocking and mumbling and turned slowly in my direction. Her eyes were bloodshot red from all the crying. Her light skin looked ashen from the tears. I felt a sense of pity for her as I took her hand.

"How do you feel? Are you okay? Can you tell me how far along you are and if you need to go to the doctor to check on the baby?" I asked each question slowly.

"Is this all my fault? Did I really just tear a family apart like this?"

I wasn't sure how to respond. I wanted to say, hell yeah, this is your fault! Instead, I smiled sweetly at her and repeated my questions.

"I'm 24 weeks and no I don't need to go to the hospital. I just need to get out of here."

"Okay. You sit here and let me check on the others. If you start to feel anything, you let me know and I will call an ambulance to come get you."

She nodded her head in agreement. I walked off from her and headed toward Rashad. Once I got closer to him, I could see his nose wasn't broken as I originally thought. The bleeding from his nose looked to be slowing down. He was still fussing and cussing.

"I hate his punk ass! Got me thinking all my life that I couldn't do anything right, and that I wouldn't ever amount to anything. Up there preaching the gospel but out here smashing little girls and married women."

"Rashad, sweetie, I need you to calm down so I can look at you," I said, gently placing a hand on him.

"I'm fine, Brooke. I've had a bloody nose before," he said defiantly as he moved my hand from him.

I sighed heavily. "*So damn stubborn,*" I thought to myself.

"Let me make sure you don't need to go to the hospital for a broken nose. I don't think you do, but I need to make sure."

"Fine," he said as he removed the towel from his face. I almost gagged from the amount of blood I saw on his face and the towel. I managed to keep my composure as I pressed around his nasal area. He winced a little as I touched him in the various areas. Once I was satisfied that he had no broken bones, I moved on to his mother. She had stopped crying and appeared to be surveying the damage to her family.

"Hi, Mama Jones," I said softly as I approached her.

"I'm sorry baby that you were here to witness all of this. I'm not sure I thought all of this was going to happen. I figured there would be cursing, but I never saw any violence happening."

"Don't you apologize for any of this! There are some things in life that aren't foreseeable. How is your face feeling?"

Although her skin was a deep mocha, the hand print from Mr. Jones was still visible. Instinctively, she rubbed her face at the spot she had been slapped.

"I'll be fine. How is Shad? Is he okay?"

"He'll be fine. Stubborn still after all these years, but he's fine."

"Good. Have you checked on his father yet?"

I was surprised she even cared to ask about him. "Um...no, not yet. I wanted to check on you before I got to him. But I'm sure he is fine."

She pursed her lips together before saying "Hmph... that's too bad."

I wasn't sure what she meant by that and I was sure I didn't want to know. I asked her if she wanted me to call the police or anything but she declined. I started to walk off to go check on her husband but she grabbed my hand.

"Brooke, I need you to grab your sister and get out of here. You've done enough. I need to get some order restored in my house."

"But I can stay. It's not a problem. I know Bree doesn't mind either. You just stay here and I'll help take care of everything."

She looked at me hesitantly but nodded her head. As I prepared to walk back into the dining room to check on Mr. Jones, I heard him yelling at Rashad. Everyone in the living room moved quickly to the dining room to see what the commotion was about. Thankfully, the two were still separated from each other, but it was obvious that they had gotten their second wind.

"I want your black ass out of my house now! You're dead to me! Ain't no seed of mine gonna disrespect me and put his hands on me!" Mr. Jones yelled at Rashad.

My heart broke as I looked at Rashad, who had tears streaming down his face. His fists were clenched.

"You ain't shit! Here I was always trying to please you. Trying to win your approval with everything I did. Nothing was good enough. I wasn't your precious Parker. I didn't play into your rules and follow your lead in ministry. But why would I if you couldn't follow the simple things like being faithful to your wife. Ain't that a basic Bible rule?"

"You don't know what you're talking about boy!"

"Oh, for real? I can remember being six and you having to make a stop at one of your parishioner's houses. Sister Latrell. Nice lady from what I remember. I think her husband was out of town or something. Parker and I stayed downstairs while you went upstairs to pray for her. I got bored playing the little games she gave us and went upstairs to find you."

Rashad looked at his mother apologetically before continuing. "Sister Latrell's door was cracked. As I got closer I could hear her moaning and you were grunting. I remember pushing the door open a little more to see what was going on. There you were on top of her. You two were so caught up that you didn't hear me slam the door shut and run back downstairs. And if you did hear, you damn sure didn't care, because it was another 20 minutes or so before you came back downstairs."

It was apparent Mr. Jones wasn't aware that his son witnessed him stepping out on his mother at such a young age. For the first time all evening he looked ashamed and hung his head.

"Then I realized this happened every time we went to pray for a woman parishioner. Mom is a good woman to you. She loved you so much. Never said a word. If you could have a good woman and treat her like that, then what hope did I have?

I always wondered why I couldn't fully love a woman, or at least treat a woman with some decency. The one woman I did love, I let her go to avoid breaking her heart. At least I had enough sense to know she deserved better, but not enough to treat anyone after her right."

The room fell silent with the exception of sniffling coming from some of the women in the room. Me included. His father sat stone faced but refused to look at his sons or his wife. Rashad wiped the tears that had been falling from his eyes and walked out the dining room. I jumped when I heard a door slam. I looked at my sister, who was sitting next to a crying Mrs. Jones.

"I'm going to leave. Simone, I highly suggest you find a ride home and get your belongings," Jerome said as he walked toward the front of the house. This set Simone off again as she ran behind him pleading her case on deaf ears.

One of the elders offered to take Simone home. One by one folks started to leave the house. My sister, Mrs. Jones, Mr. Jones, Parker and I were still in the dining room. Well, Mrs. Jones was still in the adjacent living room with Parker and Bree. I sat down in one of the dining room chairs trying to figure out what I could do.

Mrs. Jones cleared her throat. "I'm going to grab a few items and I'm going to leave. Michael you can expect to receive divorce papers."

Mr. Jones said nothing. Instead he got up and left the house through the kitchen; which was connected to the garage. Mrs. Jones proceeded upstairs to her room.

"Bree, I think we should go. We need to get ready for mom's surgery in the morning," I said softly to my sister.

Bree nodded her head. Parker wrapped his arms around her and gave her a kiss on the check, before helping her get up off the couch. We walked to our car in silence. I don't think anyone knew what to say. I sat in the car while Parker and Bree said their goodbyes. My mind wandered to how Rashad was doing. As close as we were, I never knew he witnessed his dad cheating on his mother. My heart ached for him. I couldn't imagine, nor did I want to imagine how I would feel if this was my family's truth. Especially if that truth had the power to destroy us.

Chapter 27

Natalie

I couldn't believe how fast my weekend flew by when I was in Texas. It had been a week since I returned to Atlanta and I was gearing up to start studying for my finals.

I ended up being with my mother and her sisters the entire weekend after my counseling session. Initially, I was pissed off at my mother, because she ruined my plans to see Rashad. However, the weekend turned out to be a fun one. I still would've loved to pop up on Rashad, but my mother paid for two nights at one of Dallas' most exclusive spa resorts. She even invited her two sisters to tag along and turn the weekend into a real girl's trip.

One of my mom's sisters was going through a divorce and the other one was preparing to get married for the first time. Surprisingly, the soon-to-be divorced auntie wasn't bitter and inspired me to move on from Rashad.

"So, how are you and my nephew doing?" my Aunt Cheryl, the soon-to-be divorcée, asked as we were in the lounge area of the spa resort. At the time it was the two of us waiting to be called back to our massage areas. My mother and my Aunt Diane had went back to get their massages. I rolled my eyes and sighed heavily before responding to her.

"We not. I guess," I responded flatly.

"Oh? When did that happen? Have you told your mother?"

Again I rolled my eyes before responding. "It happened about a month ago and no."

We sat there quietly for a few moments. I took a sip of my wine. I was attempting to move away from this conversation my aunt was trying to have about Rashad and I. Of course, my aunt wasn't having any of it and kept probing until I finally gave in.

"Auntie, I don't know why we aren't together. I have an idea as to the why, but I'm not sure if its really worth the discussion."

"Nat, that doesn't make any sense at all. Why are you dancing around the subject? Did the boy cheat on you or something?"

I hesitated before I responded. "Well... I don't have proof per se in regards to one situation, but I'm sure about the other one."

My aunt shook her head disapprovingly at my admission about Rashad's infidelity. I refused to tell her that I all but stalked him. Hell, I wouldn't have had to follow him around if he would have been more forth-coming in our relationship.

"That's disappointing to hear. He seems like such a nice young man, but I guess that's why they say you shouldn't judge a book by its cover."

"Yeah, I know. Trust me I was surprised myself. I love him so much and I want us to work out. The only issue is that I trust him as much as I trust sitting bare booty in a gas station bathroom."

My aunt cracked up. "Girl, you're so crazy. Honey, if you're willing to sit bare booty in a gas station bathroom then you needed to end the relationship with him."

I laughed as well and nodded my head in agreement.

"I mean why can't men do right, Auntie? I'd like to believe that I'm a good woman. Sure I have some quirks, but I've come a long way."

"That you have baby, but not all men are bad men. I'm going to share something with you that your mom and other aunt don't know." Despite us being the only two in the lounge area, she still leaned in to whisper her secret. "I cheated on your uncle."

I sat back in my chair stunned. Every time I opened my mouth to say something, I couldn't find the words. My aunt was a beautiful woman and her soon-to-be ex-husband was fine. Not only were they a beautiful couple, they were a powerful couple within the Dallas community. My aunt's husband was rumored to be the next President Obama, as long as his political career continued on the path it was going. My aunt was a powerful lobbyist for the healthcare industry.

"Is that why y'all are divorcing?" I finally managed to say.

"For the most part. I wish I had a reason as to why I stepped out but I really don't have one. He wasn't cheating on me or beating me. We've been together since college. He was my first everything and I never explored anything outside of him. I want to say I feel bad for what I did, but I think I would be lying. I actually felt liberated. Once I felt that way I knew it was time for me to leave the marriage before things got of control."

"Did you tell him?" I asked incredulously.

"Not by choice. He got suspicious and had a private investigator follow me. He confronted me about the affair and I confessed everything."

She said it so nonchalantly and without a care in the world. It was at that moment that I knew that I needed to let Rashad go. There was something about the freedom my aunt was experiencing that made me want it. Maybe one day I would get married, but maybe I should live my life until that time comes. We continued to talk until it was time for our massages.

Back in Atlanta, I hit Rashad up about coming to get the rest of my things. Instead of responding to my text, he called me.

"Hello?" I said, cautiously.

"Hey," he said, warmly. There was an awkward silence. I hadn't heard Rashad's voice since we last saw each other at his competition. "So, how are you?" he asked.

"I'm just trying to get ready for these finals."

"It's about that time."

"Yup."

"So, I know you texted about coming to get your stuff, but I think we should talk when you come over as well. I have some errands to run but I should be home by this evening. You can come around seven or so. Just hit me up when you are on the way."

"What do we need to talk about?"

"We just need to talk about some things."

A smile crept across my face. Maybe there was hope for us after all.

"Sure, Shad. I'll just let you know when I'm on the way."

"Alright then."

Once the call disconnected, I started jumping for joy around my apartment.

"I'm gonna get my man back!" I sang as I went and got myself ready to see my man.

Chapter 28

Brooke

I couldn't believe the decision I was preparing to make, but I knew that it was the right one. I had tears in my eyes as I handed the registrar my request for a leave of absence. I had already spoken with my parents about my intentions to leave medical school for the year. I wanted to be able to help take of my mother and enjoy my baby when that time came. I was going to wait until the end of the fall semester to start my leave. This would allow me to complete all my finals and rotations.

My head wasn't in the right place and I would be surprised if I finished this semester as strong as I would have liked. I'm sure that the leave would be approved because the baby was due in the middle of the spring semester and I would have missed out on some important lectures.

Thankfully, my mother was recovering well from her surgery and was at home. My father's job had been generous with giving him time off to take care of her. They even allowed him to work from home part-time as needed. Bree came home every weekend to help; while Brittany was able to help whenever she got home from school and basketball practice. I still felt I needed to be home to see about my mother. I not only wanted to help out, but I needed to be around my mother.

As I drove away from the campus to head home, I received a phone call. I answered through my Bluetooth without first checking to see who was calling. Had I checked the caller ID, I wouldn't have answered his call.

"Hello," I answered trying to sound chipper.

"Hey, are you back in town yet? We need to talk," he said in a matter-of-fact tone.

"Talk about what, Dee?" I asked with annoyance.

"We need to talk about us and the baby. I thought you would have hit me up when you got back home from your parents. Is everything alright with them?"

"They're fine. My mother was sick and now she's better. In regards to you and I, there really isn't much to talk about. The baby is doing wonderful. I will text when I have the anatomy scan. You're more than welcome to come to that appointment if you would like."

"Brooke, I know I messed up, but I really need to talk to you. Please?"

I sighed deeply. "Fine."

"Do you have time to talk today? I can come by your place or we can meet up somewhere."

"I'm on my way home now, but I planned on going back out to get lunch at the deli by my apartment. We can meet there within an hour or so."

"Okay, cool. I'll see you then. I love you."

"Uh huh. Bye."

I disconnected the call. I couldn't imagine what Dee had to say about his sleeping with Sheba. I knew that's what he wanted to talk about because why else would he blow up my phone?

As I was pondering my impending conversation with Dee, I got another call as I pulled up to my apartment. This time I checked the caller ID and saw that it was Rashad. We hadn't spoken to each other since the fight between him and his dad in Dallas. I figured that I would give him space and let him reach out to me when he was ready. I answered his call as I pulled into my designated parking space.

"Hey you," I said, sweetly.

"Hey," he said, warmly.

"How are you doing?"

"I'm doing."

"I hear that."

"So, I'm calling because I want to talk to you about everything that happened in Dallas. I was hoping we could do dinner tonight or something."

"Oh, Shad we don't have to talk about what happened. I mean unless you want to."

"Well, duh I want to," he said, sarcastically. We both laughed.

"Whatever boy," I playfully responded.

"So, can you meet tonight or do you want to do another day?"

"I actually can do tonight. Where were you thinking about going to eat?"

"Actually," he said slowly. "I was thinking about eating at my house. If that's cool with you? I can order out and bring it back to the house."

"You still can't cook?"

He laughed. "Nah. But I've perfected how to boil water without letting it go out. So, I make some mean boiled eggs."

I shook my head and laughed. "That's fine, Shad. You don't have to do anything fancy. I have a taste for some pizza and wings. Oh and can you get some ginger ale or something like that for me? I can bring some dessert if you would like."

"Nah, I got everything. Just come on by around 7:30 tonight."

"I'll be there, sir."

"Okay cool."

"You're starting to show." was the first thing Dee said as I sat down at the booth. I arrived a few minutes late because I had fallen asleep when I got inside my apartment. Had Dee not called me to let me know he was on the way to the deli shop by my house, I would have still been dreaming about Morris Chestnut rubbing my swollen feet.

"Well, I'm almost five months now, so I should be showing somewhat."

"True. You still look good." He smiled as he said that. I rolled my eyes in response and picked up my menu.

"Have you already ordered?" I asked as I looked around to see if there was a server nearby.

"No, I was waiting for you to order our food. I did order us something to drink. The server just went back to grab the drinks right before you walked in."

"You got me a sprite?"

"Of course."

"Thanks."

We fell silent as we waited for our server to come take our order. Thankfully, the server came up with our drinks and took our food orders. Once the server left we were silent again. I decided to pull out my cell phone and check my social media accounts. I didn't feel compelled to initiate conversation with him. I was going to make him work for this.

"So, how have you been?" he asked, cautiously.

"I've been doing well," I responded dryly.

"How are your folks?"

"Everyone is doing well."

"Are you planning on being short?"

I shot him a patronizing look before responding to him.

"Look, you called me wanting to talk. I can recall a time when I was trying to reach out to you and I couldn't get you to send me a smoke signal. Forgive me if I'm not being a Chatty Cathy," I said, dismissively.

He put his hands up as if he was surrendering. He was getting ready to say something but our server came back with our food. After ensuring that we had everything we needed to enjoy our meal, the server walked back off. Out of habit we said our grace together before we started eating.

"You're right. You got every right to be pissed at me. I know the way I handled everything between us was wrong. I get that now," he said in between taking bites of his meal.

I didn't say anything and continued to eat my food. When he saw that I wasn't going to say anything he continued talking.

"I'm sorry, Brooke. I really am sorry for everything. I was pissed at you for not telling me you were pregnant. Then when you did tell me you were and that you thought about aborting the baby without even telling me, I got angry all over again. All I could think about was how Sheba would threaten to abort Justice or give him up for adoption after she had him. I know you would never play games like she did, but it still put me a bad head space."

"Oh, is that why you screwed her? Because you were in a bad head space. Get the fuck out of here!" I snapped.

I surprised him with my outburst. I surprised myself with my own words, but he was starting to make my blood boil. I was beginning to think this was a bad idea and that it was probably in my best interest to leave.

As if he could read my thoughts, he said, "I didn't sleep with her. We fooled around but I swear that I didn't sleep with her."

I stopped eating to look him directly in the eyes. His eyes pleaded with mine to believe him. I chuckled and shook my head in disbelief.

"What do you mean you fooled around with her? When I asked you in Olive Garden did you sleep with her, you sat there and said nothing. If I'm not mistaken you smirked like it was joke."

"I wanted to get back at you for not telling me about the baby. Again, I know that was wrong, but I want-"

"You damn right it was wrong!" I cut him off. I heard my voice raise an octave. I took a deep breath to help compose myself. In a lowered tone, I spoke "How dare you even think that was cool? You let your pregnant fiancé walk out, emotional, thinking you had slept with your baby mama. I could have crashed or anything because I was an emotional wreck."

He hung his head low and picked around the food on his plate. I no longer had an appetite and pushed my food to the side. We sat there for a few more moments before I spoke again.

"So, what exactly happened between the two of you?" I asked curiously.

"Like I said, I didn't sleep with her," he rushed to say.

"You already said that. I asked what happened," I said with a little more force in my voice.

"She hit me up about Justice. This was the same day I learned about you being pregnant, but I hadn't spoken with you about it. Anyway, she wanted me to watch him. She dropped him off at the house and went out to do whatever. When she came to get him I had already put him to bed. I told her that he could stay the night and that I would drop him on my way out. Then we started talking and I told her that you were pregnant."

"Why on earth would you tell her that?" I asked sharply.

He stayed calm as he attempted to explain. "Honestly, I wanted advice from a woman about why you wouldn't tell me. I guess I felt the need to tell someone."

"Because your mama wasn't available to talk to?" I said in disgust.

"Brooke," He said, quietly. He tried to reach across the table to grab my hand. I folded my arms across my chest as acknowledgement to his gesture. He quickly took the hint and continued speaking.

"Brooke, look I'm not sure what happened, but we started kissing and she went down on me. Had Justice not woken up when he did, I'm almost sure we would have slept together. The night we went to Olive Garden I was supposed to get up with her but I cancelled after you left. I couldn't go through with it. She was pissed at me. I haven't seen Justice in over two weeks. I do love you and I cannot imagine life without you. I know I messed up, but let me make it up to you and prove to you that I will be there for you and our child."

Hot tears streamed down my face. I closed my eyes and shook my head. This man was unbelievable. I breathed in deeply, held my breath for a second, and slowly released it. When I opened my eyes to look at him, I could see the remorse in his eyes. In my mind he was too late, but my heart wanted to give him another chance to prove his sincerity. However, the Bible says the heart can be deceitful and mine was trying hard to deceive me.

"You are unbelievable, Donovan. I needed to hear this that night at Olive Garden. I don't know what to say."

"Say you will give me another chance. I love you. I want you to be my wife. I want us to be a family and raise our child together as a unit."

"I think that ship has sailed, Donovan. I love you, too and a couple of weeks ago I wanted to be your wife. Despite the fact you were acting like a jerk. I held out hope for us. But what you did with Sheba and the reason why…" my voice trailed off as I shook my head in disgust. "I can't see how we can go back."

He put his head down in defeat. The part of me that loved him felt bad for him but it was time that I started putting myself first and that I protected my heart.

"Look, I know I put a lot out there. Why don't you take a few days to think about it? And if you're sure that you want to move on, then I will respect your decision. I'll still be there for you and the baby, but will you at least think about it?"

He looked pitiful. I could tell he wanted me to say yes, even if I didn't mean it.

"I'm not sure there is much to think about. I love you. I really do love you, but I think it is best if we end this now and focus on how we can co-parent."

"So, that's it?" he asked dully.

"I'll come get my stuff later this week and I'll bring your stuff with me," I said as I rose from the table. I placed some money down on the table to pay for my meal. He looked at the money as if it was poison.

"You know I can pay for this, right?"

"I know, but I got me today. Look, I'll text you the information again for the anatomy scan."

When he didn't say anything I walked out the restaurant with my held high and a burden lifted.

Chapter 29

Rashad

You're dead to me!

My father's statement kept replaying in mind as I attempted to study for one of my upcoming finals. I was in one of the quiet rooms in the library. Although it was quiet where I was, my mind wouldn't shut itself down to focus on the task before me.

It had been a week since I had spoken to anyone from my family. I did leave a message on my mom's phone letting her know that I had made it back to Atlanta, but other than that I hadn't spoken to anyone since my return.

Parker called or texted me daily, but I didn't know what to say to him. My mother reached out to me a couple of times. She too received the silent treatment. I couldn't process if I was mad with my mother for how things played out at the house or embarrassed by everything that happened. In frustration, I pushed my books to the floor. I let out a deep sigh as I rubbed one of my hands down my face. I realized my feeble attempt to study before my dinner with Brooke wasn't going to be fruitful. As I picked up my things to prepare to head back home, my phone vibrated on the table. I looked at the caller ID to see it was my mother calling me. I debated on if I should answer her call or not. I quickly decided to answer and avoid her calling in the cavalry to see if I was alive.

"Hi, Mom."

"Hey son."

The sound of her voice instantly soothed me. Her simple greeting was filled with love and warmth. Instead of leaving the quiet room, I sat back to down to speak to my mom.

"How have you been, son? I got your message when you made it in but after that I didn't hear from you."

Guilt crept up on me when she said that. It hadn't been my intentions to avoid speaking with her or my brother.

I told her as much and added, "I didn't know what to say Mom. I didn't know if I was mad that you didn't tell me what you had planned or if I was pissed that I allowed myself to lose control. To be honest Mom, it was a lot."

"Shad, I couldn't fathom your father responding the way he did. I've seen your father get really angry before but never have I experienced him getting violent. Shoot, he never used that type of language around me. Well, not since he got saved and had given his life to Christ."

I scoffed at her latter statement. "Do you really believe that dad knows Jesus?"

I heard her chuckle before answering. "I do. Your dad was on fire for God. There was a true anointing on his life. But sometimes with power and money…" her voice trailed off.

We sat quietly on the phone for a while. I imagined my mother was thinking of the good times past with my father. I, on the other hand, was thinking of how much I hated this man for the things he did to my mother and how he could rip apart our family in the way he did.

"Son, I want to apologize," my mother started.

"Apologize for what, Mom?" I asked confused.

"For your father. Never in a million years would I have guessed he would take you and your brother on his trysts. I suspected he had stepped out a few times in our marriage, but I never had concrete proof. Just a feeling."

"Did you ever confront him?"

"Every time. He would deny and he would act differently. He would become more attentive. It would last for a while, until it didn't last any longer. He would always do enough for me not to fully question him. I just knew he was cheating, but I loved your father with all that was in me and I wanted our marriage to work." She paused as I heard her blow her nose on the other end. Then she continued.

"I wanted it to work son, but the final straw was when you said he took you guys with him. I was done with him after finding out about Tasha and Simone, but in case I was still holding out hope, it died when you said you saw him in bed with that woman."

I felt warm tears fall down my face. I wish I was there with my mother to hug her and tell her in person that I loved her. I heard her sigh on the other end.

"Anywho," she said as she sniffled. "The divorce papers have been sent to your father. I'm staying with your Aunt Val until I can figure out my next move."

"Okay Mom." was all I could manage to say.

"I love you, son. I know you're probably concerned, but I- no we, are all going to be alright. God is still very much in control despite how it looks and how it feels right now. And when your brother calls you, please talk to him. He is worried sick about you. Okay son?"

I laughed. "Yes, Mother," I said in a playful, exaggerated voice.

"Seriously!" she said with a laugh.

"I tell you what, Ma. I'll call him when I get off the phone with you. I got to run and get some food, but I'll give him a call."

"Alright son. I love you and I'll talk with you soon."

"Love you too, Ma."

Instead of calling Parker right away, I placed an order for the pizza and wings for my dinner with Brooke. As I left the library Denise accidentally ran into me, dropping her books. She managed to hold onto her cell phone which was the reason for her running into me in the first place.

"My bad," I said apologetically, even though I wasn't at fault for our collision.

"Yeah, your bad. Are you going to pick up my books or not?" she asked rudely.

I wanted to kick her books across the library. Instead I adjusted my book bag, smirked, shook my head, and kept walking to my car. She had me fucked up if she thought I was going to help pick up her books and she had an attitude. Apparently, my actions pissed her off as she said a few choice words to my back.

I decided to stop at the grocery store to get something to drink and the dessert. I still had a couple of hours before

Brooke would get to the house. My phone vibrated as I walked into the store. I reached in my pocket and saw I had text from Natalie telling me that she was going to be coming closer to 7:30 or 8:00 due to her study group.

Shit. I thought to myself. I forgot I told her to come get her stuff today. Not only did I forget, I told her to come close to the same time as Brooke. I had to figure out a way to get Natalie to come over another day. I sent her back a text and kept shopping. I didn't check my phone again until I got in the car.

I'm not going to be able to come any other day. Today is the best day for me. I can come earlier or later though. But this week is a bad week for me.

I read her message at least five times. Each time hoping that an epiphany would come to me. If she came earlier it would be better, but if I knew Brooke she would be early. She had always been a stickler for time. The only thing that seemed logical was to have her come later when Brooke left. I sent back a response and hoped it all worked out.

"I want to thank God for allowing me to be here today and come before you all. It has been a trying week for my family and I," the man said as his voice choked. He looked as if he was trying to force tears to fall from his eyes, but none would.

He closed his eyes and prepared to say something else. Before he could speak again, another man approached him and whispered something in his ear. The man that had been speaking before opened his eyes and balled his fists.

"It appears that there are some who would like for me to step down, but I refuse to step down without telling my tru-"

His microphone was cut off, but he could still be heard yelling about getting his truth out. At this point four men came and attempted to escort the man off the stage. They surely thought the irate man would leave peacefully and without further incident.

When one of the men went to grab the irate man's shoulder, he threw a hard left hook and connected with the other man's jaw. The people in the building began to scream and shout as the five men wrestled. Eventually, the four men were able to subdue the irate man and remove him from the stage.

My father's pastoral career was officially dead with a two-minute video. I had spoken with Parker when I made it back to my apartment. After he cursed me out for avoiding his calls and texts, he told me what happened the following Sunday at our father's church. Apparently, the elder board started their investigation into the accusations against my father the day after the eventful dinner at our house. As part of the investigation, my father was placed on leave until it was completed. My father, being the prideful man he was, not only showed up to church but took the microphone from the assistant pastor. All hell broke loose after that and that video was played across all the local Dallas news stations.

I called my brother back after I watched the video for what had to be the tenth time.

"You watch it?" he asked as soon he answered the phone.

"Several times. I'm still in shock," I replied.

"Man, the phone won't stop ringing here at the house. I'm glad Dad hasn't been home since this all went down. Mom told me to come to Aunt Val's house with her, but I told her I think I'm going to look into getting my own place."

"I don't blame you, man. That's crazy. Dad has really fallen off."

"Yeah man, but let me let you go. I gotta prepare for my seminary class tonight. Let me know how everything goes with you and Brooke tonight."

As soon as I got off the phone with Parker, I heard a knock on the door. I went to the peephole and saw Brooke standing on the other side. I opened the door to let her in. Brooke wore a pair of jeans that had tears in the thigh area and a loose fitting soft blue top. Her hair was cascading down past her shoulders. I leaned in and gave her hug. I felt a little bulge in her midsection, but I was distracted.

I breathed in deeply as I took notice of her vanilla scent sprayed on her neck. It took everything in me not to kiss her or allow my hands to roam her body.

"Do you mind if I use your bathroom?" she asked as she took off her ballerina looking shoes at the front door.

"No, it's right down the hall on the right side. I'll bring everything to the living room."

"Oh, good because I'm starving."

We began eating as soon she returned from the bathroom. Initially, we ate in silence and not looking at each other. There was an awkward tension between us. It had been years since we had been alone with one another. Years ago we would have been laughing and talking, but we weren't teens anymore and I took for granted the amount of time that had passed between us.

"Soooo," she stated, curiously.

"Yeah," I said, softly.

"Are we going to talk or are we just going to sit here…" she made a face while raising her palms upward, as if to ask what's up.

"Right. I did bribe you over here for a reason," I said, chuckling. I was hoping to break up the tension.

She smiled and chuckled before responding, "Food has always been my weakness. So this was a good bribe."

It happened again. The awkward silence was back. I took another bite of my pizza and a sip of my drink. I could tell Brooke wasn't going to offer any conversation. I couldn't blame her because it was me who called her.

"I want to talk about what happened with my dad. More specifically I want to talk about what I said."

She put her drink down and gave me her full attention. I took a deep breath before continuing.

"I know you hate me for how things ended between us."

"I don't hate you, but I-" she quickly tried to interject.

I made a skeptical face at her before I spoke again. "Brooke, let me finish what I got to say."

I could tell my statement annoyed her but she grudgingly nodded her head. Once I was satisfied that she wasn't going to keep cutting me off, I continued.

"Look, I didn't really realize how deep my issues ran with my father until we fought. I knew I was messed up and no matter how much I tried to not be like him, I found myself slowly becoming him. I love you, Brooke. I have always loved you, but I was going to hurt you if I stayed with you. Now, I know the way I went about our breakup was jacked up, but blame that on my immaturity. I apologize for that and I apologize for hurting you the way I did. Believe me when I tell you that I couldn't love you the way you deserved, let alone give you everything you deserved."

Brooke had tears running down her face. I gently wiped at her tears. I then placed my hands on top of hers. She gently squeezed my hands. I waited patiently for her to respond.

"Rashad, it wasn't until you said that you still loved me at your parents' house that I was able to fully forgive you. Once you said what you saw your dad doing, I understood why you broke up with me. I carried so much hurt and anger in my heart against you for years and I hope you can forgive me for how I handled things after we broke up. I never gave you a chance to even apologize. In my mind you were dead to me. I wanted nothing to do with you and I literally did everything I could to erase you from my life."

"I don't blame you for how you handled things. I ain't never been dumped, so I don't know how I would have responded."

She laughed and wiped at a stray tear. "Oh, you got jokes?"

I laughed and playfully raised my hand in surrender. Then I grabbed her hands again and pulled her closer to me. I leaned in and kissed her on the mouth. When she didn't pull back, I attempted to deepen the kiss. I heard her slightly moan as I moved my hands to wrap around her waist. All of the sudden her body jerked as if a bolt of lightning struck her. She quickly pushed me back and moved to the edge of the couch.

"I can't. I mean we shouldn't do this," she said breathlessly.

"Did you and your fiancé get back together?" I asked confused.

"No. We're definitely not together." She paused before continuing, "But I am pregnant."

My mouth dropped opened. That explained why she had thickened up and the bulge I felt when I hugged her earlier.

"Pregnant?" I finally managed to say.

"Almost 20 weeks. I was pregnant when you saw me at the Greek picnic."

I scratched at my head and sat all the way back on the couch. I didn't know what to say to her. When I didn't say anything, she got up and started walking to where she had placed her shoes and purse.

"Wait, Brooke. You don't have to leave or anything. I'm just shocked. I don't know what to say."

She stopped putting her shoes on and turned to look at me. I motioned for her to come back to the couch. She hesitated for a moment, but sat back down next to me. She kept her eyes focused on her hands until I gently turned her face to me. I softly kissed her on the lips again.

"I love you, Brooke, and I'm not about to lose you again. I know we have a lot to work through and whatnot, but I'm not about to run off because you have a baby."

She smiled. "You're sweet, Shad," she started. "But don't you think you should be with someone who doesn't come with baggage?"

"It is 2010, almost 2011. Everyone has baggage. I got daddy issues and you got baby daddy issues. We'll figure it out. I mean if this is what you want to do?"

She sat thinking for a minute.

"And what about Natalie? What is going with you two?" she asked, skeptically.

"Natalie and I are definitely done. Matter of fact, she's supposed to come get her stuff. Plus I feel the need to talk to her. I figured I owed her an apology as well."

She scoffed at my last statement.

"What's that for?" I asked.

"Why would you apologize to her? For what?" she asked indignantly.

"I mean I wasn't necessarily boyfriend of the year. I did some things to her that she doesn't know about, but I want to have a clean conscious. This is what my therapist suggested."

"Therapist?"

"Yeah, I called one not too long after I got back in town. I had my first session yesterday. I figured I should talk to someone about my issues with my dad. Maybe I'll be able to fully get over everything."

The look on her face told me she was surprised, but impressed.

"You know it's hard for black men to talk to anyone about their problems, let alone go out and seek professional help. That's great, Shad. Seriously." She briefly paused before continuing. "Look, why don't we do this? Let's take it slow. We're both getting out of serious relationships and a lot of time has passed between the two of us. I think it's best if we rebuild our friendship first and see where things go from there."

I nodded my head in agreement.

"That makes sense. I guess we don't need to rush into anything. I don't know if you're crazy or not."

"Ha ha," she said sarcastically. "That would be your girl, Natalie."

I laughed as we both stood up and walked to the front door.

"I'm going to get out of here before Natalie shows up. She is far from my favorite person and I cannot see her being excited to see my face over here. Even if you two aren't together."

"That's probably a good idea."

"But first let me go to the bathroom. This bladder of mine has a mind of its own since being pregnant."

I smiled as I watched her walk down the hallway. Despite the bomb she dropped on me, I was pleased with how our talk went. I wasn't sure how to process her being pregnant. I wanted to believe that I could handle it and be there for her, but if I was honest with myself I wasn't sure. I'm glad that she suggested we take things slow as opposed to us jumping back into things as if we didn't break up almost a million years ago.

I was startled out of my thoughts as a knock came at my front door. I did a quick glance at my watch and saw it was a few minutes after the time I told Natalie she could come get her stuff. She knocked again with a little more force when I didn't answer after her first knock. I quickly looked down the hall to make sure that Brooke wasn't on her way back up front.

As I opened the door, I could hear Brooke coming down back the hallway. I started to slam the door shut, but it was too late to dodge the collusion that was taking place.

Chapter 30

Natalie

I arrived to Rashad's a few minutes later than the time he told me. I had sent him a text letting him know that I was running late due to my study group going longer than I had anticipated. One of my professors was giving us a take home final before the Thanksgiving holiday break. To ensure there wasn't any cheating, my professor grouped us into four and gave each group of four a different version of the final.

I didn't think anything of Rashad not returning my text as I made my way over to his place as we planned. I was anxious and didn't know what to expect when I got over there. I had so many thoughts running through my mind. What if he wanted to get back together and work through our issues? How would I respond if that was the case? I imagined that I would be ecstatic. However, I wouldn't make it easy for him. He would have to prove that he wanted to be in a relationship with me.

As I got out of my car at Rashad's, I walked past a vaguely familiar white Lexus RX350. At the moment I couldn't place where I had seen it, but I was sure that I knew the owner of that Lexus.

When Rashad answered the door, all thoughts of the Lexus went out of the window. Rashad looked absolutely gorgeous wearing a pair of plain gray sweats and an Emory law t-shirt. His locs were pulled back into a neat ponytail and he smelled divine. I was so enthralled by his looks that I didn't notice I was still standing outside waiting to come in.

"Umm?" I said, taking a step forward towards the door.

I was taken aback when he stepped outside and closed the door behind him.

"What's up?" he asked, trying to sound nonchalant. The look on his face said he was nervous as hell about something.

I made an annoyed face at him as I crossed my arms over my chest.

"I'm here to get my stuff and to talk," I said slowly to him as if he spoke a foreign language.

He nodded his head slowly as if he was trying to search his memory of our earlier conversation. This pissed me off and I was becoming increasingly annoyed with him. Why was he acting as if he didn't call me to come get my stuff and to talk about God knows what?

"Rashad, what the hell is the problem? You called me to come get my stuff and said you wanted to talk to me. Are you going to let me in or what?"

"This isn't a good time. I know you said that you couldn't meet up any other day, but I can bring your stuff to school or drop it by your place."

"Excuse me?"

"I'm tired and I really need to get in bed. I got a long day ahead of me tomorrow."

I stepped back and took a deep breath. I knew his ass was lying and I was determined to find out why. I pretended to be cool with what he said and acted as if I was going to leave.

"Oh, okay. Well, yeah...why don't you do that? Go get some rest. I'll text you when I'm home and we can figure out a good time for us to meet up."

His face showed relief. "Cool. Thanks for being so understan-"

Before he could say another thing, I quickly pushed past him and opened the door. I couldn't believe who I saw sitting on his couch. Brooke jumped as she turned towards the door to see me standing there. I started to walk towards her, not sure what I was going to do once I got close. Before I could take any steps, I felt Rashad grab me by the arm.

"Natalie, this isn't a good time. I promise we'll talk," he said firmly.

I whipped my head back and forcefully tried to break free from his grip but he refused to let me go.

"You're a liar!" I shouted at him. Not caring that his front door was open and that his neighbors could probably hear what was going on.

"Natalie, don't do this. This isn't what it seems."

With my free hand I slapped him across the face. This forced him to release my other arm. He looked at me with fire in his eyes. For a moment I thought that he was going to hit me back.

"You're a liar. I asked you if you knew her and you said no. Do you remember that? The way she danced on you that day at the Greek picnic and how close you were to her." I shook my head in disbelief as I remembered our argument about Brooke. "But if you don't know her why in the hell is she at your place?"

I started to slap him again but he quickly grabbed my hand and turned me around so that I was outside of the door.

"You need to leave. Now!" he barked.

"I fucking hate you, Rashad and you tell that bitch Brooke, I got something for her, too!"

I stormed down the stairs to my car. When I got to my car, I opened the trunk to grab my baseball bat. I kept a bat in my car for protection and tonight wasn't an exception. I walked over to Brooke's Lexus and began to put in work on her driver's side window.

"Hey, what are you doing?"

I dropped my bat to the ground as I turned to see a couple out walking their dog. Instead of responding, I took off running to my car. I was thankful that I had push to start and didn't have to search for any keys.

I threw my car into reverse and skidded off into drive once out of the parking spot. I was in such a rush to get away from Rashad's place, that I didn't see the lights until it was too late.

Chapter 31

Brooke

Tears flowed down my face as I watched Natalie smash the windows on my truck. I was standing on Rashad's patio wishing I had a way to stop her that didn't put my unborn child at risk. I cringed with each swing she took and with each hit I became angrier and wanted to kill her. If I had only left when I said and not went to the bathroom, I could have avoided all of this.

Rashad came outside on the phone with 911 reporting Natalie. When he hung up the phone, he put his arms around my waist from behind.

"I'm so sorry for all of this, Brooke." His voice dripping with remorse.

I turned to face him with a bit of contempt. I felt my abdomen cramp a little and took a few deep breaths. I started to respond but turned back around to see Natalie running back to her car after a couple walking their dog asked what she was doing.

"Great. She's going to be fugitive," I said, rolling my eyes and shaking my head.

"Well, I have her address so it isn't like the police can't find her," Rashad said.

We stood on the porch watching her speed out of the complex. The couple that was walking their dog was still standing on the sidewalk in front of my truck. The man tried to take off running and get a picture of Natalie's license plate number, but she was gone before he could grab his cell phone out of his pockets. The lady appeared to be on the phone as well. I assumed she was calling the police as well to report Natalie.

"I hope she doesn't get into an accident driving like that," I said as I walked back to the patio doors of Rashad's place.

"Me neither. Let's go down and look at the damage," Rashad said, gently placing his hand on the small of my back.

Before we could get out of his apartment good, we heard it. First, there was a screech of brakes and then the loud sound of metal colliding together. Rashad and I took a quick look at each other. I developed a sinking feeling in the pit of my stomach. Without another word, we ran through his apartment and out the front door.

Thankfully, he lived on the second floor and it didn't take long to reach the bottom of the stairs. In front of us we could see the couple who had been walking their dog running into the direction of the loud sound. While I was running, I began praying that it wasn't what I thought. I prayed that my nemesis hadn't been involved in an accident.

My stomach lurched as I saw Natalie's driver side door completely pushed in by a large SUV. The airbags in each vehicle had been deployed and there appeared to be no movement.

"Oh my gosh!" I heard the lady with the dog yell. The man with her tried to calm their dog, who was whining and panting in a circle.

I looked over to Rashad who was squatting with his hands to his head. He kept opening and closing his mouth as if he was trying to scream but it was muffled by shock of the scene. I patted my pockets for my cell phone and realized that my phone was in Rashad's apartment.

I asked the man with his phone out to call 911 to request an ambulance. Because it was around ten in the evening, traffic was light as most people were probably at home for the night. I went to Natalie's car and tried to open her passenger side door. The door was unlocked and I was able to get in the car to check on her. She was bleeding from her head and she appeared to be unconscious. I didn't want to touch her too much but I needed to check for a pulse.

I breathed a sigh of relief as I was able to detect one in her wrist, albeit it was faint, she was still with us. I could hear the sirens blaring as I stepped out her car and made my way over to the other vehicle. By now the occupants had gotten out the SUV. I cautiously approached what appeared to be a mother and her teenage son. Both looked to be fine physically, although the son appeared to be in a bit of daze.

"Hi. My name is Brooke and I'm third year medical student at Morehouse. Are you and your son okay?" I asked gently.

The mother's pale face was streaked with tears. She pushed her brunette hair back behind her ears as she took an assessment of the scene.

"I tried to tell him to move into the next lane, but she was coming out so fast that all we could do was slow down and brace for the impact," she said in a shaky voice.

"Is she dead?" her son asked in a stressed tone. I looked at him with pity. I could tell that he had never witnessed anything like this.

"No, she isn't dead," I said, placing a hand on his shoulder.

The ambulance pulled up to the accident, along with the fire department who began blocking off lanes of traffic. The police had also arrived at the same time. I introduced myself to the emergency personnel and informed them of Natalie's condition. The emergency crew quickly moved to get Natalie out of her car and onto a stretcher. As they tended to the other family, I made my way back over to Rashad who was still sitting in the same position. I sat down on the ground in front of him and gently grabbed his hands, placing them in mine.

"This is all my fault. I should've asked you to come another day or something," he said as tears rolled down his face.

"Rashad, this isn't your fault. You can't take the blame for this," I said in a calm and even tone.

"Brooke, she could be dead because I couldn't remember what time I told you both to come over. She wouldn't have damaged your car. She wouldn't have left upset and emotional had she or you come another day. All I wanted was for her to get her things, apologize for how I treated her, and move on. I was trying to right all my wrongs in one day."

I sat silently for a moment and looked down at the ground. I tried to search for comforting words to give him, but none came to mind. In a sense I could understand how he felt her accident was his fault, but I also knew that everything happened for a reason. I wasn't sure what the reason could be for all of this happening and I wasn't sure I wanted to know the reason either. Then I realized that someone needed to call her mother. That someone had to be Rashad.

In a voice barely above a whisper I said, "You need to call her mother."

He didn't respond. Instead his breathing became quickened as he closed his eyes. He began to take deep breaths in an attempt to calm what appeared to be an oncoming panic attack. I repeated again that he needed to call her mother.

"And say what Brooke?" he snapped at me. He opened his eyes and looked at me with disdain. I gently squeezed his hand and gave him a half smile.

"Tell her that her daughter has been in a bad accident. That she needs to get here as soon as she can to see about her. She will ask questions about what happened to which you can let her know that you can explain everything when she gets here, but that it's important she get here."

He looked past me as if he was searching for an answer amongst the accident. He sighed deeply and stood up. Rashad reached down and helped pull me up to my feet.

The couple with the dog was talking to the police and began pointing at us as we walked in their direction. A female police officer began walking in our direction.

"Hi. I'm Sergeant Taylor. Are you two witnesses to this accident as well?" she asked once she was in front of us. She was a tall, beautiful cocoa brown sister. Her hair was neatly pulled back into a tight bun.

We both shook our head.

"We actually called the police initially due to one of the victims vandalizing my car," I answered.

Her eyes widened at my statement. "The couple over there said that this accident was probably a result of that. So, you are the owner of the damaged vehicle?"

"Yes ma'am," I responded solemnly and began giving her my statement of what happened prior to the accident. Rashad stood there quietly and answered questions as they were asked of him. I held his hand in an attempt to keep him calm. I could tell he was embarrassed to tell the officer what happened, but she didn't appear to pass any judgment as she took our statements. If she had any judgments she was great at maintaining a poker face.

After we finished giving our statements, we went back to his place to grab my stuff and head to the hospital to check on Natalie. While in route, I called Rochelle to inform her what happened to her cousin and to let her know that Rashad had already called Natalie's mother. Rochelle agreed to meet us at the hospital.

When we arrived we were told that Natalie was in emergency surgery. Because we weren't family, the nurse wasn't able to give us any additional information into

Natalie's condition. Frustrated, we found a couple of seats in the waiting room. We didn't speak to each other while we waited for her surgery. Rashad closed his eyes and I heard light snoring coming from him.

I was preparing to text Rochelle to see where she was, but I spotted her walking into the ER waiting room. I could tell she had been crying by her red puffy eyes. She still had on her pajamas and her hair was still in pin curls. I must have called her as she preparing for bed. We hugged each other tightly. When we broke our embrace I could see a fresh set of tears on her face.

"Brooke, this is crazy," she started. "Her mother would die if she lost her."

"We weren't able to get much information on her because we aren't her family. Maybe you can talk to the nurse and get an update."

"Yeah, let me do that. I spoke with her mom and she is booking the next flight out of Dallas and should be here in a few hours."

She hugged me one more time before heading to the nurses' station. As I got ready to sit down, I felt a trickle run down my legs. Then I felt a pop and rush of water. I began to cry out for help as my water broke.

"I named him after my grandfather, Edward. Isn't he handsome?" I asked Rashad showing him the picture of the baby.

Rashad smiled at me as he gently patted my hand. It was the next morning and we still were at the hospital. All the stress from the previous night had caused me to go into preterm labor. Because my water broke I was forced to deliver my son nearly 10 weeks early. Due to the spontaneous nature of the labor and him being so early in the gestation period, his viability was pretty nonexistent. He was a fighter though and lived for about two hours after I had him.

I held him and cried the entire time. I told him that I loved him so much and how I wish I could have gotten to know him. I swear I saw a smile on that little boy's face.

He passed away in my arms. I still held him until I drifted off to sleep from the medication. When I woke up he had been removed from arms, but the nurses had placed him in a bassinet next to my bed. I held him one more time. I made sure that I kissed every little finger, toe, and all over his face. I took a couple of more pictures of him before letting the nursing staff know they could take him.

"Now, I have to make funeral arrangements for my child." I felt tears beginning to form in my eyes. "How am I supposed to plan for that?"

Rashad didn't say anything, but continued to hold my hand. We sat silently holding hands as I cried all over again thinking about the passing of my son. I quickly let go of Rashad's hand when I heard Donovan come into the room. He hadn't noticed Rashad and I holding hands as he rushed to my bedside. I had called him this morning to inform of Edward's passing.

"Baby, I'm so sorry this is happening!" he cried, kissing my forehead.

I felt myself slightly cringe at his kiss, but quickly remembered this was his loss as well. I gave him a half hearted smile.

"It'll be okay," was all I could manage to say.

"Brooke, I'm going to go see about Natalie. Her mother should be here and I know she has a boatload of questions. I'll check up on you a little later," Rashad said as he prepared to leave my room. He reached out to Donovan, in an attempt to shake his hand. Donovan hesitantly shook his hand.

"I'm sorry for your loss, man," Rashad said and walked out of the room.

An awkward silence came over the room once Rashad left. I knew Donovan wanted to know who the hell Rashad was and why was he in the room with me. Before he could ask any questions, I volunteered to share with him who Rashad was.

"Rashad is a friend of mine. His brother and my sister actually date each other. Yes, we used to date as well before you ask and no he isn't the reason we aren't getting back together."

Donovan nodded his head as he processed the information I shared with him.

"So, did he bring you to the hospital or something?" he asked trying to sound nonchalant.

"Actually, we were already here at the hospital because his ex-girlfriend got into an accident."

Again he nodded his head as he processed. I could see in his eyes that he wanted more information but I wasn't in the mood to talk about the events that led to me being admitted in the hospital.

I wiped at a few stray tears and sat up a little straighter. I winced a bit as the pain of my cesarean stitches threatened to open up if I didn't move more slowly.

"So, we have a lot to do regarding Edward's arrangements. My folks said they would take care of everything for us. We'll just need to decide if we want to bury him here or Dallas. I told them more than likely here since we both live here and it would be easier."

I said this to Donovan as if we were sitting in coffee shop and talking about the weather. His eyes briefly became downcast at the mention of having to plan our son's burial.

"I don't know, Brooke. It's all a lot right now. I've never been in a situation like this. When my pops passed it was different. You know? Just let me know what you decide and I'll help out in whatever way I can."

I nodded my head. We talked for a little longer until my medicine kicked back in and I dozed peacefully back to sleep.

"This was beautiful, sweetheart," my mother said hugging me tightly.

I embraced her back and closed my eyes as a few tears escaped. It had been a week since my son passed away. I decided to have a small and intimate memorial service for him. My parents, sisters, along with Donovan's mother and sister attended the graveside service. Even Rochelle had attended. I reached out to Rashad about the service, but I didn't receive a response from him. We hadn't spoken since the day he left the hospital after Donovan had shown up.

"Do you want to get something to eat, baby girl?" my father asked me while rubbing my back.

I lifted my head up from my mother's shoulder and nodded my head. With my sisters in tow, we began moving toward my parents' rental to figure out what to eat. I started to walk past Donovan who was standing talking to his mother and sister. It was obvious that he was having a hard time dealing with the loss of our son.

"Hey, I will meet you guys at the truck," I said to my folks.

I spoke and hugged Donovan's mother and sister. After a little small talk with his folks, they excused themselves and waited for him in the car. We stood silently looking toward the site where Edward was buried.

"Seems surreal," he said, barely above whisper.

I nodded my head in agreement at his statement.

"Yeah. What a way to get introduced to parenthood. I never thought I would ever birth and lose my child on the same day," I said as I wiped at a stray tear.

Donovan turned to face me. The whites around his hazel eyes were bloodshot red. I reached up to his face and gently placed my hand on his check. He closed his eyes and leaned in closer to my hand. He took my hand and kissed it sweetly.

"What do we do from here?" his eyes searched mine for an answer.

I shrugged my shoulders and softly said, "I don't know."

"I'm supposed to leave for the military in a month. We were supposed to be planning…" he dropped his head and his voice trailed off.

"Planning our wedding," I finished for him.

He looked at me again, this time with slight contempt. I felt a wave of guilt rush over me. I was heartbroken over my son's death, but relieved that the relationship I shared with Donovan was dead.

Since I had a week to prepare for the memorial service, I also had time to think about my relationship with Donovan. It was during that time that I realized that I had been dating who I thought he could be; his potential.

Yes, he was a good father to his son and he treated me well, but he worked a dead end job, chased a rap career, and couldn't complete an associate degree. By the time he decided to go into the Air Force, I had mentally checked out of the relationship. If I hadn't gotten pregnant I would have turned down his proposal and walked away from him months ago. If I was honest with myself, I should have walked away when he didn't tell me about Sheba and went missing after she gave birth to Justice.

"Yeah, we were supposed to get married. Be a family." there was a hint of bitterness in his voice.

"Life has a funny way of changing our plans," I said, wiping more tears away.

His face softened as he leaned down to kiss me on the cheek. I smiled at him.

"I will always love you, Brooke."

"And I will always have love for you. We are forever bonded."

"Well, let me get out of here."

"Yeah, of course. I hope everything works out with you and the Air Force. Give my love to Justice."

He didn't respond. Instead he leaned down again and this time kissed me softly on my lips. I gently kissed him back and replayed the good times in my mind. I felt another tear fall from my eyes as I literally kissed my past goodbye.

Part 3
The Aftermath

Chapter 32

Rashad

Epilogue 2 Years Later
Fall 2012

I hung up the phone, excited. I had successfully negotiated my first multi-million dollar entertainment contract. After months of negotiations with a hard nose network attorney, I was able to secure a lucrative deal for my client. He was an up and coming actor set to star as a headliner in a new sitcom. I was stoked! I had to tell someone the good news before I burst, so I picked up my office phone.

"Hi baby," she said sweetly into the phone.

"Hey babe. What are you doing? Did I catch you at a bad time?" I fired off.

Her background was loud but I could hear it growing silent as she moved into a much quieter area.

"I'm in between classes so you're good. What's up? You sound excited about something."

"Brooke, baby, I closed the deal on the Jamison contract!"

"Oh my gosh, sweetie! That's freaking awesome! God is so good!"

"Yes, He is, baby! But the best part of this deal is that I get ten percent upfront for his signing bonus." I heard her squeal with delight as I told her the anticipated amount.

"Wow! Do you know what that means, babe?"

"What?" I asked as I began to loosen my tie from around my neck.

"It means that I can finally stop going to medical school and buy a medical degree off line," she laughed before continuing, "No, but seriously baby. You about to blow up! Talk about favor."

"It ain't fair but it sure does feel good. It's going to feel good putting that tenth in the offering bucket."

She laughed and I joined in with her.

"Well, look babe, I gotta run. I have one more lecture for the day. Thankfully, today is a short day and I get spend some time with my husband."

I smiled when she said the word husband. "Aight, cool babe. I'll see you in a little while. I love you, Mrs. Wallace and rub that belly for me."

"And I love you, Mr. Wallace. The babies say they love you too, Daddy. We'll see you later on at the anatomy scan."

I hung up the phone on cloud nine. I couldn't believe how much my life had changed since the night of Natalie's near fatal accident. By the grace of God, she had survived. She slipped into a coma for about three weeks. When Natalie woke up, she discovered that she was paralyzed from the waist down and suffered some memory loss. After her release from the hospital, her mother withdrew her from school and moved her back to Dallas to start an aggressive rehab treatment. From my understanding her mother shelled out big bucks to place her in one of the top rehab centers in Dallas.

It took her nearly a year to relearn everything and from what I hear she still struggles from time to time. Her mother initially blamed me for everything that happened that night. I couldn't blame her either. Had I been more aware of what I was doing, I would have never invited Natalie over that day. I would have waited or I would've brought her stuff to her. I still can't explain why I was holding on to her belongings. It took a lot of prayer and counseling for me to cope with everything.

Brooke was with me every step of the way. For a while I stayed away from her because I felt responsible for her losing her son. She ended up attending my graduation and came to my apartment with my brother. Parker made some lame excuse about having to go somewhere and left Brooke and I alone.

At first we didn't talk to one another. At one point I even tried to lock myself in my bedroom, but she wasn't having any of it. She said one powerful statement to me that night, that snapped me out of my self pity.

"I don't blame you for what happened."

From there we talked about everything. We talked about my father, her relationship with Donovan, her son's funeral, and everything in between. For the first time I was able to be transparent and vulnerable. I didn't care if she judged me or not, but she didn't. She listened to me. Brooke encouraged me to keep seeing a therapist to help me process everything regarding my family and my relationship with Natalie. She even got me back into church. I met her with some resistance, but I slowly gave in.

My life changed when I attended a men's group one evening. The men there came from all different walks of life but they had a passion for God that I hadn't seen in a long time outside of my brother. The more I attend those meetings, the more I wanted to experience that passion these men had for God. They were unashamed and unafraid of their faith in the Lord. I gave my life to Christ in one of those meetings and my life hasn't been the same since.

I still don't know how Brooke was able to be there for me while dealing with the death of her son. She still went to grief counseling for his death but after about year or so she was able to share her story with other women who had experienced a loss.

After the burial, she re-enrolled into medical school at the urging of her parents. They insisted that she not come back to Dallas but instead focus on finishing her medical degree for the sake of her son. Initially she protested but requested that her leave be removed and that she be granted admission back in the spring semester. This proved to be a positive move for her as it allowed her to shift her focus and now she was almost guaranteed to finish at the top of her medical class. I couldn't wait for her graduation to come this spring.

As for my family, things were different back in Dallas. My parents' divorce became final, after a messy fight over assets. My mother ended up prevailing in the divorce and made out nicely once the dust settle. Not as if she needed anything from my father. I believe she wanted to prove a point.

My father was never ousted from the church after his fiasco in the pulpit. It wasn't for lack of trying by the elder board, even though the investigation by the elders found him guilty of all the accusations. It's hard to put someone out who founded the church. As a result, my brother finally stepped out on faith and started his own church taking half of the congregation with him. In an attempt to distance himself from our father, he started a non denominational church in Arlington, with the help of my mother and Brooke's family.

As I grabbed my things to get ready to meet Brooke at the doctor to see our twins, I stopped by James's office to tell him the good news. James and I decided to go into private practice together after we graduated law school. I didn't think it was going to work at first because things were going so slow, but God has a way of turning things around.

"Hey man. You got a minute?" I asked when I got to his office.

"Yeah, man. I need a distraction from this brief," he said, pushing back from his desk.

I quickly filled him in what happened with the client. By the time I finished telling him, he was jumping up and down. He and I knew that this was going to be enough to put us in the black. "Praise God!" He said, giving me a high five.

"He is good! But let me run. I got to meet Brooke at the doctor. We are going to find out the sex of the twins today."

"Alright, man. Hit me later and let me know what the doc says."

When I made it to my car, I sat there for a moment to reflect on everything. I couldn't believe all I've been through over the past two years. I didn't think I would be able to recover after the fallout with my dad and Natalie. After the storm there is always sunshine. My sunshine was my wife, the soon to be mother of my children. Yeah… I can dig it.

ACKNOWLEDGMENTS

Lord, I love you. No, seriously Jesus. I. Love. You. As I write this I get chills because You have blessed with me an incredible gift. For the longest I've tried to walk away from writing, but You never gave up on me. You dropped this story on me and I couldn't help but share it with others. My prayer is that You will be glorified, that the lost will be found, that forgiveness will take place and that You will be pleased. May I never forget who I work for.

Lutis, my loving husband, thank you for being a team player! Thank you for being my support system. It's not easy being married to an attorney and an author, but you do it well. Much credit to your parents for raising such an honorable man. I love you always and forever!

Mommy, your mind is brilliant! Thank you for pushing me, for being my cheerleader, and for believing in me. We did it honey!

To my daddy and step-mom, thank you both for all your love! The words of encouragement that were always on time. I love you both!

To my siblings- OJ, Steven, Monet, and Kenni, remember I am the favorite! But I still love you guys. Lol!

Oh and Shortie, Mesha and Bree, you all already know I am the favorite. Lol!

My unofficial reading committee- Domonique, Jocelyn, Mary, Andrele and Nikki. You gals rock! Your feedback throughout the process was everything! Especially when I wanted to give up. Thank you all for being a part of my journey!

To my editor/publisher/friend/everything in between, Christian- we first have to thank V for bringing us together. Who knew a blogging group would be the catalyst to finally push my dream forward. Thank you for taking a chance on me, and for believing in my story.

And to my friends and family- thank you for sharing in this journey. It would take another book to thank everyone. But you know who you are. You know the role played in my life. You have been instrumental in this journey.